THE RITES OF SPRING BREAK

The Point Pleasant Holiday Series

SHANE K. MORTON

❀ Created with Vellum

As always this is for my husband. We will never need a second chance as we have always relished our first!

KRIS (THE PAST)

Walking across the stage to get my diploma is probably the most important thing that will ever happen to me in my entire life! Well, except for becoming Hunter's boyfriend. That is definitely more important than a rolled-up fake diploma, even if it is a momentous occasion.

I have been released into the great wide world.

Finally. I feel like I've waited for this moment my entire life.

It's like my entire body is humming! There is something electric about starting the second part of your life. I've always thought about it this way. Years one through four do not really count. You're just learning to be a person when you're that young. But the moment you step into elementary school, you begin part one of your life. Part two is college. Psychologists say that the growth level that you experience in college is leaps and bounds above any other years of your life. Some people take four years during this phase, and others get their doctorate and take ten to twelve years to finish it. I am planning on four.

I have a lot of plans, at least that's what Hunter says. He tells me that I am the most driven person he has ever met. I believe it. I think it's good to know who you are, where you're going and what you want out of life. I know it all. I have life planned to the infinitesimal, which means Hunter's life is planned too. Life without him would not be a life I would want to live. He is everything to me, just as I am to him.

I look out over the vast lake from the pedestrian bridge that sits above the small lagoon. It really is a bridge that makes no sense. It goes from one patch of sand to another, but here is where Hunter and I had our first kiss two years ago. I can still feel the pressure of his lips against mine, the memory of it is that important to me. It changed everything. He went from being my best friend to so much more in the span of twenty seconds. Our kisses last a lot longer now.

"Hunter, damnit..." I look at my watch. He's late.

I sat down on the bridge and dangled my legs between the metal railings. I watch the gulls dive towards the water in search of fish. They are usually successful. I find it fascinating. A few of the early arrivals for the graduation bonfire are hanging around on the beach, laughing, and being totally obnoxious. I see a few of Hunter's football player friends passing the ball back and forth while they wait for the sun to go down about thirty minutes from now.

That's why we were meeting on the bridge. It's going to be a beautiful sunset tonight. The sky is clear, and as the sun sets behind the mountains, magic will happen in the sky. It always does this time of year.

"Kris!" I turn and see Hunter jogging towards me. His broad shoulders carry his varsity jacket well. I probably should have brought my own jacket. But the bonfire will warm me up, if Hunter doesn't. He makes his way over the bridge quickly, barely winded from his jog. "Sorry, babe. Mom wanted me to talk to my cousins, who came in from Vermont. They're a handful."

"I figured it was something like that. Is your mom still on for family graduation dinner tomorrow night?" I ask, dreading the whole affair. I'm not a big fan of being in the spotlight. That's Hunter's job. He was born for it.

"Yeah. She loves your Aunt Sally and wouldn't miss it for the world. You know we have some of her photos in Mom's office. We're big fans." He slides down beside me and wraps his arm protectively around me, pulling me close. I lean my head on his shoulder, and he kisses the top of it.

"Are you going to miss The Pleasant?" I see him shrug. I know he will. "I don't think I'm going to. I can't wait to get to LA and start the rest of my life. Our dreams are coming true, aren't they, Hunter?" I smile, knowing that I only have another couple of months here. It's not that I hate it. I don't, not really, but Point Pleasant has never really felt like home to me. We moved here when I was in middle school, and even though everyone is nice, and the school was great, I miss being in a large city. We moved from San Francisco so Dad could be closer to his sister. I adore Aunt Sally, just like everyone else in this town. But I am also excited to leave.

"Yeah, of course, I will. It's my home. But it's not like I'm leaving it forever, is it? I mean, we'll probably move back here when college is over. I can start my own animal hospital, and you can work for your Aunt. You know she would love you to run her gallery one day." His soft breath tickled my neck as he told me his dreams. Our idea of the future didn't mesh well, yet. But I would win him over to my way of thinking, eventually. I always did.

"Anything can happen," I chirp happily, trying hard to ingrain this memory, so it becomes a part of me forever. Hunter and I staring out onto the water as we talk about our future. He is the most important part of my life, and I cling to him as I would a life-raft, afraid that if I ever let him go, I would be swept away and lost forever. "Promise me, Hunter... Promise me that nothing will ever change."

I hear him sigh, his muscular chest rising with his slow intake of breath, his heartbeat steady and calm as he kisses me again on my head. I snuggle deeper into his shoulder, smelling his clean scent and fading cologne. "I promise, Kris."

How was I to know that he had lied to me? How could I know that I wasn't enough to keep us together?

The days of summer flew by in a blur. We made out on the dock, in his barn, and in the back of his truck like we couldn't get enough of each other. Our kisses were full of passion and fire, our hands unable to stop touching each other, grasping at holding onto what we had, even if time would be our undoing.

The summer faded, and it was time for me to start school. I kissed him and said a quick goodbye in my driveway. Hunter and my parents waved at me as I started my drive to California and the life I had always wanted. He was supposed to meet me a month later.

He never came.

Of course, I called him. I begged for him to change his mind and come to Los Angeles with me, but no matter what I said, all he ever replied with is, 'I cannot hold you back. I love you too much.'

I waited a year, hoping he would change his mind and realize that he needed to be with me as much as I did him. I cried almost every night of my freshman year. Eventually, I locked him away in a secret compartment of my heart, so he could never hurt me again.

My parents moved to Seattle, and I never saw him again. That was ten years ago.

KRIS (PRESENT DAY)

"Can you answer that damn phone?" Cassandra screamed from the other side of the cubicle. She screamed a lot, and her voice was as shrill as a damn banshee. It echoed against the acoustic ceiling tiles, which were supposed to absorb sound and make the office a quieter place.

It didn't work with Cassandra.

Amber rolled her eyes and raised her middle finger in a gesture that we all understood before she picked up the phone. "Good afternoon, fine arts department, how can I help you?" She sounded happy, but she was anything but.

"Kris," my boss's voice made me jump. "Can I see you and Cassandra in my office, please?"

My stomach sunk. Whenever Donna Jean Marcus, the dean of the department, asked you into her office, it was rarely with good news. I grabbed my notebook and pushed myself back from the desk that I had started to feel chained to. It wasn't that I didn't like my job, I did, most of the time, anyway. But as I got promoted from adjunct professor to tenure track, the pressures and demands of working in the art world were starting to cause me bouts of angina.

Like I said, I liked my job. I just thought I would be in a different place within the art world. I had stopped making art, and now all I did was teach students who would rarely do anything with their talent besides becoming a high school teacher. I always had my eye out for that one student that might change the course of popular art and find themselves one day within the history books or hanging in the Louvre. I was about to give up. My students, well, most of them, anyway, could care less about breaking the mold and making something new. They just wanted to pass.

I didn't even really give myself an honest shot at trying to make it with my talent. After a year of the hustle and bustle, I found myself at a crossroads. I had shown in some LA galleries and had even sold a few pieces, but I wasn't making a living wage. The struggle was real, and I needed to find a job that would give me free time to still pursue my dream. A college had an opening, and I had the right connection to interview and show my portfolio. So, when it was offered, I jumped at the opportunity. Teaching is a lot more time consuming than I had assumed. I now only showed my work at faculty shows. Collegiate life had put the final nail in my dreams of taking the art world by storm.

My Aunt wasn't thrilled with my new career path, either. I spent the last six years knowing I had let her down as well as myself. The trouble with comfort and stability was it was hard to leave and jump into the unknown. I was not a very brave risk-taker, and the older I got, the more scared I became.

"What do you think the dragon lady wants?" Cassandra seethed as she stood outside my small cubicled office. "More budget cuts?"

"If they cut us any harder, we won't have jobs," I huff, worried that she might be right.

"Hell, we won't have a college," she smirked at me. "Come on. Let's not keep her waiting. I really don't want to see her breathe fire today."

I followed Cassandra down the corridor, her heels clicking on the tiled floor. She knocked and smiled broadly as Dean Marcus looked up from her desk.

"Good. Come in and shut the door, please," she ordered tersely. "I really don't want Amber spreading this around."

Cassandra strutted to the far chair, and I shut the door behind me, my stomach in knots. I was going to be let go, or worse, she was adding to my course load. Either way, it would suck. I took the closest chair and crossed my legs. Cassandra winked at me. She knew I was a basket case and thought it was endearing. She was twisted.

"So, I'm just going to cut to the chase," she took off her glasses and gently bit the earpiece as if she were pondering the cruelest way of letting us go. "Professor Marsden has decided to retire at the end of the semester, so it seems we will have an opening. You're both on the full-time track, but this position would be full tenure for one of you. On paper, you are neck and neck. Both of you are published and have worked as full-time artists, with your work being shown in good galleries." She smirked at us condescendingly. Dean Marcus had work that hung in major museums. It was ugly and overtly modern, but she was there. *We* weren't, and she enjoyed reminding the other professors that we weren't on her level. It was a great management style... not.

"I think we will make our decision after the faculty show this spring. Seriously, you are both quite good teachers and artists in your own right. Professor Marsden was life drawing, and we will have to replace his classes with a new adjunct, but this is a chance to create a legacy here with your own genres.

I look forward to being wow'd by both of you. Don't let me down. That's all. You can leave the door open," she waved her hand, dismissing us.

We stood up and filed out of her office in shock. Tenure? It's what I had been working so hard for, wasn't it? Why did it make me feel so cold?

We walked back towards our small office spaces, and Cassandra touched me on the shoulder.

"Kris? Holy shit," she whispered incredibly loud. I put my finger to my lips and grabbed her hand, pulling her into one of the small lecture rooms around the corner.

"Holy shit!" she exclaimed, a wide grin spreading across her face. "Can you believe that? I never thought the old buzzard would retire."

I sat down on one of the art tables and pulled my feet under me and crossed my arms. "This is a big deal for one of us," I stated flatly, understanding that this meant we were in competition against each other. We had been friends for years. She was one of my besties, I could feel my brow furrow.

"Stop it," Cassandra demanded. "I can see the anxiety spreading across you like a shadow. It's what it is, Kris. You and I are both fantastic at what we do, and we just need to be ourselves and do the work that we always do, okay. I'm still your biggest supporter, even though I'm gonna do my best. I expect the same from you, you know."

"I do." I forced my shoulders down away from my ears. It hurt, that's how knotted my muscles were. I wasn't the best at handling stress and never had been. I was too type A, and when things went down a different path than I had planned, it took me a while to roll with it. "I... I want it because I want the money and the security, but I am also afraid of what it means, Cass. If I get it, I have officially given up on my dreams. That's a hard pill to swallow. I don't want to be stuck, and I feel incredibly stuck, right now."

How can you make a decision about your future, when you have no idea what it is you want?

My phone buzzed in my pocket. I pulled it out, which felt like a win. My pants were tight, and I really had to work to get it free of my pocket.

Shit. It's my parents. They never call during the day. I swiped.

"Hi," I said quickly, worried that something had happened to one of them.

"Honey, we are so glad that we got a hold of you," Mom was using her soothing voice. Yeah, something was wrong.

"What's up?" I asked. A shiver shot up my spine as I heard her sigh. "Honey, it's Aunt Sally. She passed away over the weekend. Dad and I are catching a flight down there this afternoon to get her ashes."

"Oh God... Aunt Sally?" I questioned, hoping that it wasn't true. She was a wild child, even as a senior citizen. It didn't seem possible. Numbness crawled over my body.

"Yeah... I know, honey. She apparently had cancer and didn't want to tell anyone. It came as a shock to us too. We just spoke to her a couple weeks ago. You know how she didn't like to be a bother to anyone. Are you okay, Kris? I know how close you were to her," Mom was trying to be calm and composed. She was the only one in our family who was reasonable with her emotions.

Aunt Sally and I were really close. Then I moved away. I hadn't seen her in a few years. Not since she flew into Seattle to spend Christmas with the family. She had even made the trip to LA a couple times to see me, but I had never gone back to The Pleasant to see her. Guilt set heavily in my soul.

"I can... uh... Let me see if I can get a flight out. What time is the funeral?" I stuttered, fighting my emotions back as hard as I could.

"Honey, there's no funeral. You know Sally. She wanted a

memorial during the summer underneath her large oak tree in the back yard. So, we will go back then and give her the sendoff she deserved. Honestly, honey, there's nothing you can do, and besides, I know you have work." I hate it when she still made decisions for me as if I were still a child. But I didn't say anything. She was right. I had three more classes to teach this week, and two of them had mid-terms, so it wouldn't be the best idea to traipse off.

"Fine. I guess you're right. I just can't believe it, Mom... I can't believe that she's been sick and didn't tell any of us. Dammit..." If I had called her more often, would she had shared this with me? Probably not. Aunt Sally was a very private person. We were so much alike, it was scary.

"Oh! I almost forgot. Her lawyer called today and asked for your number. So you should hear from Mr. Bennarde sometime soon, I guess. Are you sure you're okay? I hated to call and tell you this, sweetheart. I know how much you loved her. Her sun rose and set around you, Kris." Mom said sweetly. I heard Dad's muffled voice in the background. "Okay, honey. Sweetie, I'm going to have to let you go. Your father says he loves you, but he is a mess right now. I have to help get his bag packed. I think we're gonna stay for a couple days and we will call you when we get there. I love you, Kris."

"I love you too, Mom," I answered before ending the call and setting the phone down on the table.

Aunt Sally...Fuck. I spent the rest of the day thinking about all the ways I had let her down. Regret for not seeing her more often, for not calling her more, for giving up on my dreams overwhelmed any thoughts I had.

When I got home, I pulled out what little photos I had of us. My favorite was one that Dad had taken of us in her art studio. I was covered in paint, and her head was thrown back with laughter. Her eyes sparkled with mischief, just as they always did. Aunt Sally was fierce. It was inconceivable that she was gone. How can someone so vibrant and full of life be cut down with the fucking disease? I cried as I held our photo. Tears splashing down upon my t-shirt.

I thumbed through the rest of the photos. They were all happy memories, even the ones with Hunter in them. She used to call us the Three Musketeers because we spent so much time in her studio or at the gallery.

I couldn't believe I would never hear her laugh again.

3

HUNTER (PRESENT DAY)

"**Y**o! Hunter, you want that last slice of pizza?" John slapped me on the back before picking it up and stuffing it into his mouth. As usual, he didn't even give me a chance to reply. Nothing stood between him and a slice. It had become a joke at the station.

"No, you go ahead," I laughed easily. It was good to laugh. The last few months had been quite hard for me, and any chance to laugh, I happily accepted. Between work and caring for a sick friend, I was exhausted. Now, I just wished I was that busy again. "You look like you need all the carbs you can get."

"Asshole," John said with his mouthful. "We can't all be a walking wall of muscle, like you dude. Some of us are challenged by our metabolism."

"I think some of us just refuse to go to the gym," I teased. Here at the search and rescue station, which also served as The Pleasants fire station, we had a state of the art gym in our building. Being in shape was important for what we did. Most of the guys didn't use it, though. I did. "I'll be happy to work out with you, John. Maybe help you get rid of the flab your wife's always teasing you about."

"She likes it. There's more of me to keep her warm at night," he grinned as he wiped his hands on his pants, the pizza grease glistening on his pant leg. "Besides, I have two kids. Who has the time to work out as much as you do?" He picked up the remote and turned on the TV to some stupid reality show he always watched.

I rolled my eyes. They all had the time, the other guys just didn't like working out. They were in good enough shape; it wasn't like I felt my life was at risk because of them or anything. But I took my job, and my health seriously, always had. I was a football and rugby player in high school, and I liked being muscular and knowing that I was the best that I could be. I had bulked up over the winter and would soon start a shred for the summer. Besides, working out helped me get through all the emotions I tried to bottle up. I had gotten quite good at hiding my angst.

"Whatever, dude," I sat back in the chair and put my hands behind my head, making sure my biceps flexed. "I can't believe you watch this shit. What's it called again?" I stared blankly at the TV screen. It was mind-numbing, and I understood the dumbing down of America. This trash on TV, right here, was the cause.

"It's called, Marry A Stranger. They don't get to see each other until the wedding day. It started off with only texting, then phone calls, then childhood photos, and today they get to go on a scavenger hunt to learn more about each other. The wife loves it, and I've gotten hooked." John grimaced. "It's bad, I know, but I can't stop myself from watching it."

Before I could say anything else, our doorbell rang. I stood up and walked out of the room and down the hallway to our small lobby. I saw her through the glass door and beamed at her. Mrs. Markle had brought us some baked goodies. She did this every so often, and we all loved her visits.

I opened the door, and she winked at me. "Good afternoon, honey. I made some of my famous dump-truck cookies for you, boys. I remember how much you liked them in school, Hunter." Mrs. Markle really was the sweetest, and everyone in town adored her. Hell, most of us had her in at least one English class when we were in high school.

I took the plate from her outstretched hands. "Thank you, Mrs. Markle. You know how much we appreciate you for these. Would you like to come in?" I held the door for her.

"No, honey, I have too much to do today. How are you, Hunter? I haven't gotten a chance to say anything to you since I heard the news. Bless her heart. Sally was a beautiful and kind soul, and her loss to the community is tragic for all of us. But how are you, honey?" She reached out and touched my arm. I could feel the warmth from her hand as it radiated up my arm. There was just something about Mrs. Markle that made you feel seen and loved.

"I'm doing okay, I guess. It... well... After the year we had... I guess I am a little lost. I've gotten so used to helping take care of her that I feel as if something is missing, besides her. Sally was really good to me, and I was glad that I could be there for her, but I'm also glad it's over. It got really bad towards the last few months, and I hated seeing her so frail." I bit my lower lip. It was still raw, and I didn't want to vomit my emotions all over Mrs. Markle. She, like everyone in The Pleasant, saw me as this strong man who could deal with almost anything, and I didn't like breaking the illusion. I know it's stupid...

"She loved you, Hunter. You are a wonderful young man, and I'm sorry that you had to go through that, but I am glad that she had you there with her. I know how much it meant to her. Now, you go and eat those cookies. They help fill the void... trust me," she waved as she turned around and walked down the sidewalk towards her parked car. "See you later, Hunter."

"You too, Mrs. Markle," I called before shutting the door and leaning against the wall. This last year had aged me. Watching someone, you care about go through that damned disease was a horrifying experience. Sally had no one here for her, and we had gotten very close over the years. She was the one to help me through the breakup with Kris, even if she did think I was being an idiot. She had become like my own aunt, and I cherished the time we had together, even if the last few months had been brutal.

"I have cookies," I called out as I walked back down the hallway and into the living quarters. John jumped out of his chair and rushed me. Rhys slid down the pole, and before I could even set the cookies down on the table, they were being devoured by the guys. "You are all animals."

"Takes one to know one," Rhys said with his mouth stuffed with gooey goodness. "Damn, I love it when Mrs. M stops by. Sometimes when I'm alone, I dream of these cookies."

"She should open a cookie shop!" John exclaimed as he reached for another. "I know she bakes for her guests at the bed and breakfast, but these deserve their own storefront. Aren't you going to have any?" He looked up at me, concern heavy in his eyes. They all understood what I had been going through, even if I kept most of it to myself.

"Nah... I'm meeting Sam for coffee in a few minutes. Call me if you need me. I'm still on call for another couple of hours. Hey, you two, save some for the other guys, okay?" I admonished, knowing there would only be crumbs left when the next shift arrived.

"Yes, boss," Rhys' snide voice made me want to pull the cookie from his hand. He had been getting on my nerves a lot lately. Not really his fault, we just didn't have anything in common. He's the kind of guy who never takes anything seriously and in this job that's dangerous.

"Alright, I'm out. Don't get into any trouble," I called over my shoulder as I headed out of the small firehouse. I walked into the cool spring air and felt the gentle breeze run through my hair, blowing my bangs down into my face. I needed a haircut. The trees were beginning to bud, and the yellow spring flowers were shooting out of the ground.

It was a fool's spring. April in The Pleasant still brought snow onto the mountains and passes even if the days in town had warmed up. There was still a lot of danger to the skiers. Melting snow was dangerous terrain, and you never knew when a slide could happen. Thank God this year has been relatively calm. We've only had to rescue people for their own stupidity and not nature's wrath.

I entered the town's park and walked by the fabled gazebo. Like many teenagers in this town, I have snuck up here to see if it would tell me the name of the person who would hold my heart. And like every teenager who has ever tried it, I heard nothing. I grin as I pass by, remembering the thought that crossed my mind when I met Kris. If I had known him, then, would I have heard his name? I shake the thought from my head as soon as it happens. If I had, it would have been a lie, even if he has never left my heart.

I pick up the pace and turn the corner. Margie's Coffee Shop sits halfway down the block. I pull my light grey wool jacket tighter. The wind is cutting through me as it zips between the mountains and empties onto this street.

As I open the door, I catch Sam and Crystal laughing about something that one of them must have said. Her cackle fills the room, but I catch Sam's eye, and he smiles at me and stands, opening his arms so I can give him a big bear hug. He is so much smaller than me. Most people are.

"There he is. I quit writing over an hour ago, you know. Crystal has been keeping me entertained with gossip." He reaches around me, and I envelop him in my arms, picking him up and squeezing him.

"Sorry, Sam. I let the time get away from me. Besides, I'm technically still on duty, you know." I sit down beside him.

"You want your usual, handsome, and would you prefer the non-leaded version?" Crystal winks at me.

"Yeah, better give me the decaf, Crystal. I'm gonna go home and pass out. I just pulled a sixteen-hour shift, and I cannot sleep in those beds at the station. John snores like he's a fucking chainsaw." I shrug. It's not like I can do anything about it. We only have a pair of beds there, and someone needs to stay awake, so it might as well be me.

"Aw... I was hoping I could get you to go out and have a cocktail with me at Rumours tonight. All the other gay boys are occupied with their baby daddies. Well, except for Wally, but he's away at a conference. It's drag queen bingo," she says hopefully, her eyes twinkling with mischief.

"You know I would love to, babe, but I also have to go back to pick up Finn from the station. Besides, I am beat, Crystal. Raincheck?" I smirk at her. Crystal is cool. She knows just about everyone in town, but her specialty is the gay boys that she adores. We all love her right back. She's like our very own therapist/advice columnist. She's rarely wrong.

"Yeah, yeah. Alone at the gay bar again. You boys are starting to give me a complex. Maybe I need to start hanging out with some girls," Crystal says seriously. Sam and I look at each other and burst out laughing. "Hey, it could happen." She smirks.

"And Hunter could also find a boyfriend." Sam slaps me on the back. I know he's joking. It still stings. The comment, not the slap.

"Okay, we are not getting into that again. I think with

Sally's passing, I might be able to finally put Kris behind me. I need support, not jibes." I grab Sam by the arm and squeeze gently. If I hadn't been hung up on my ex for the last decade, it's possible that we may have become something more than friends one day. But that ship has sailed long ago. He's become one of my dearest friends, though, and I am grateful for him.

"Okay, bitches. I need to finish cleaning this place so I can close. I'll be back in a bit. Scream at me if anyone comes in," Crystal says gruffly as she heads into her kitchen.

Sam looks over at me and frowns. "Are you okay? I meant to check in with you yesterday, but I had Lilly's parent-teacher conference, and Grayson couldn't go. Guess who went with me?" he snickered.

"Don't tell me you and Marc went together?" I laughed because that shit was funny. It's not often in this world that your ex-boyfriend has the possibility of becoming your step-son. That could only happen to Sam.

"Yep. It was kind of fun. We're getting along great, actually. He prefers to be called Clay now, though. I know... I still have a hard time not calling him Marc. But I'm glad we're getting along so well. I guess stranger things have happened." He nudges me with his shoulder. "They might happen to you too."

"The only thing I am hoping for right now is to fall asleep as soon as I fall into bed." I stood up and kissed him on the top of his strawberry-blonde head and ruffled it before I stretched, a low moan escaping my lips. I was beat. "Speaking of, I think I better get out of here, or I may not make it back home. Damn, I feel like I haven't slept in days."

He reached out and grabbed my hand. "Did you see them?"

I sighed. "Yeah. They came in to collect some of Sally's things and to take her ashes back west. Her memorial will be this summer, I guess. It was what she wanted. She always said that summer here in The Pleasant was the most beautiful summer in America."

Clay smiled as he let the thought settle. "I think she's right. Was seeing Kris' parents tough?"

"No. They were as great as always. I mean, it's been a while, but they were as wonderful as I remembered. I was uptight about it because I wasn't sure if he was coming in, you know? He couldn't make it. Figures." I gripped the back of the chair and could feel my knuckles tense. "It's better this way, Sam. Probably for everyone. Ok, I really gotta go."

Sam stood up and gave me a quick peck on the cheek. "Okay, Hunter. I'll see you later this week, though, right? Maybe we can surprise Crystal and take her out for a drink or something. She's been grumpy because the only person that's been around to hang out with her is Tad, and I think she's over it."

I waved over my shoulder as I turned around. "Sounds like a plan. I'll call you tomorrow." I walked towards the door, my feet feeling heavy. Fuck, I still had to walk back to the station.

"Love you," Sam called.

I turned around and smiled at him. "Love you too, Sam."

I opened the door and walked out into the chilled air. It had gotten dark outside, and I pulled my jacket tight and zipped it. Finn was waiting, and so was my bed.

4

KRIS (PRESENT DAY)

I have a ton of regrets. But none of them have weighed on me as heavy as Aunt Sally. All of the times, I chose to do something else besides visiting her, played through my memories. I was a shitty nephew. She was the reason I had become an artist, and I owed, pretty much, everything I was to her. Her care, love, and guidance had shown me who I was meant to be.

I think I have lost part of that now. Fear and comfort had made my artistic needs take a backseat. That was something I owed to myself, as well as Sally, to re-evaluate and take a good long look at what path I should plant my feet firmly on. Life was something you were supposed to enjoy, not dread, and recently I had not been finding happiness in what I did.

Mom and Dad had flown back from The Pleasant yesterday. They said they had a nice trip and saw quite a few of their old friends while they were there. I wanted to ask them if they had seen Hunter, but I wasn't even sure if he was still there. Maybe he had finally found someone and moved away to his own someplace else. Maybe he had gotten fat...

I chuckled at the thought. We would probably colonize

Mars before that would ever happen. Hunter was obsessed with health, at least he had been. I had no idea who he was now.

Today was the last day of school before a well-deserved week off. The students were all talking about their plans to go to Aruba or Cozumel. I was planning on eating pizza and trying to figure out what I needed to do to wow the dean at the faculty art show. Sadly, I had no ideas. My artistic vault was drained, and all I could think of was pedantic and boring. I really needed to find something that was original and would make the committee see that I was an artist that they wanted to secure for the college. That was what I wanted... maybe.

The buzzing from my pocket shocked me out of my pondering. I pulled the phone from my pocket and looked at the screen. I didn't know the number, but I knew the area code. I slid right and put the phone on speaker.

"Hello?" I said quietly.

"Mr. Bolton?" an older gruff voice asked. "This is Harry Bennarde, from Bennarde, Benson, and Associates, I am the lawyer for Sally Bolton's estate. Is this a bad time to talk?" He sounded world-weary, and from the type of call he was making, I could understand why. Dealing with death always takes a toll on the living.

"Yes, Mr. Bennarde, this is Kris Bolton, and I am available now. Honestly, I've been dreading this call. My mother said you needed to talk to me. What's this about?" I asked, a cold feeling creeping over my body. I didn't want to have this conversation.

"Well, Ms. Bolton's will has finished probate, and we are now able to distribute her possessions as she saw fit. A collection of her artwork will be donated to galleries, and the rest, it seems, now belongs to you. That would include her house, studio, and gallery, all of which she owned outright, as well as her monetary assets and the possessions inside all buildings.

Ms. Bolton was a popular artist, and I must say I was a big fan of her work and of her in person, of course. She was a remarkable and kind lady. I was sad to hear of her illness, and I am truly sorry for your loss." He breathed heavily into the phone. I felt the weight of his words like a vice on my heart.

"I'm sorry... She left everything to me?" I asked. My brain was already in turmoil, and this was not computing. Me? I felt the tension trickle from my shoulders. Of course, it was me. Aunt Sally had no children, and Dad was her only brother. It made sense. I was always special to her as she was to me. This was her last gift. I wiped the tears from my face and tried to compose myself. I was failing.

"What," my voice cracked. "What do I need to do? Sorry, this... I am surprised... I mean... I didn't know and..."

"I understand Mr. Bolton," he sympathized, his voice soft and understanding. "When can you come to sign everything? That would be the next step, and this would have to be done in person. Sally said you were a teacher? Would there be a time in the near future where you could make the trip?"

"You're in The Pleasant?" I asked, knowing the answer already. Aunt Sally was a big proponent of keeping things local.

"Yes. I understand if you need to postpone, Mr. Bolton, however, everything would stay in holding until you are able to come here to sign. It was a stipulation in your Aunt's will," he explained, and it hit me. I had to go back to Point Pleasant after all these years. The thought of having to go back there without her...

"One second, please," I managed as I put my phone on mute and let my emotions get the better of me. The tears flowed fast, and I tried to catch my breath. I didn't even realize I was hyperventilating until I was in the throes of it. I grasped the table and steadied myself as best I could, concentrating on the things I had control of. My shoulders, my legs, my hands, and finally, I took a long slow breath and felt myself slowly coming back from my grief.

I wiped my eyes on my t-shirt and laid my head back against the chair's soft cushion. I felt my breathing return to normal, and I unmuted the phone, now that my emotions were back in check.

"I will fly in this weekend," I said slowly. "Spring break begins tomorrow, so this is probably the best time, as I had no plans except staying home."

"Then it looks like you're coming home," he said sadly. I didn't correct him. The Pleasant had always just been a stop in my life, never my destiny. "I'm sorry it's under these circumstances. I can meet you at my office tomorrow. Let me give you my personal cell so you can call me when you arrive. If you get in too late, I will be happy to meet you Sunday, if necessary. Do you have a key to Ms. Bolton's house? I imagine you will stay there?"

"I don't," At least I didn't remember having one. "I will try to find another place to stay. I'm not sure that I could handle that, right now." I answered, honestly. "Could you suggest a place for me?"

"Sure. Do you remember Mrs. Markle? I'm sure you had her as your English teacher when you went to high school here. She now owns a bed and breakfast. It's a delightful place. Would you like me to send you the information?"

"Mrs. Markle..." I remembered her kind tutelage. She was one of those teachers that you remembered, for all the reasons a teacher strives to be remembered for. "Of course, yes, I think that sounds perfect. Can you email me, please?"

"Of course. I know you have a lot to figure out today, so I will let you go, Mr. Bolton. What is your email?"

I gave him my address and quickly checked my point balance to see if I could use it for my flight. I found a trip that would get me into Denver by noon, which meant I would arrive in Point Pleasant by dusk that afternoon if I drove. A small commuter flight would get me across the lake, so I chose that. I would take the helicopter across and be in town a couple hours earlier, that way. I didn't really need a car, did I?

I buttoned up my plans and walked into my bedroom. I had to pack. But more importantly, I had to get myself ready to go back, mentally, and emotionally. I had no idea what might lie in store for me in The Pleasant except pain and grief.

5

HUNTER (THE PAST)

Watching Kris drive away, almost killed me. I wanted to run down the street and make him stop. I needed him to turn around so bad and to tell me that he couldn't leave without me, couldn't stand to be parted from me. My heart thundered in my chest, it's rapid beat causing anxiety to rush in and tunnel my vision to the point I almost cried out with fear. I was terrified. But my fear was that I would lose him.

He waved as he turned the corner as he went away from Point Pleasant, away from me. I knew what this meant, even if I didn't want to admit it. Kris had a destiny, and it wasn't here, but this was it for me. The Pleasant was my home, and I knew that if I went with him, his dreams would be forever lost. In the end, he would follow me back here, and the regret of coming back would tear us apart. He would resent me, resent our life, and I couldn't have that for him. He deserved more than this place, even if, to me, it was where I wanted to be. For him, it would be death. It would be the end of us, and I couldn't let him settle for something he didn't want just because he loved me.

If I followed him, his dreams would come to a crashing end.

I fell to my knees and buried my head in my hands. I felt a gentle caress through my hair, and I let my emotions flow. Tears streamed down my face and pooled into my hands that hid my emotions from everyone else, though it didn't fool them. They saw. They heard my sobs.

"Shhh... honey. It's going to be okay. You guys can go on in. Hunter and I are going to take a little walk," Sally said as she twirled my hair around her hands. She knew. She always knew. Sally was uncanny with her precognition, and I often teased her about her witchy ways, even if I secretly wondered if it might be true.

I heard the Bolton's front door shut and knew that Sally and I were alone. She knelt down in front of me and held me as I tried to calm my tears, doing everything I could to pull myself back together and failing with every try.

"It's okay, Hunter. There... there... sweetheart, you just let it all out," she soothed as she embraced me tightly. Her curly hair tickling my face as I dropped my hands and sobbed onto her shoulder until I had no tears left. Her hands stroked my wavy hair and made small patterns on my back. I felt my spent body relax into her. As always, Sally had a way. My body listened to her and calmed itself, even if my heart was breaking into pieces.

"I'm sorry, Sa...Sal...ly," I managed to say in between quick gulps of air. I wasn't a crier. I was usually steady and in control. This was against my core being, even if it felt right at this moment.

"Oh, Hunter... You think you're the only one who knows, don't you?" she whispered into my ear, causing chills to rush down my spine. "I know what it's like to love and lose too. But you haven't lost... not really. You just have to make the right choice. You two are meant to be together, I've seen it, honey, I know."

I buried my face deeper into her shoulder, closing my eyes as tightly as I could to prevent them from betraying me again. I was afraid that if I let myself go, again, I might never stop.

"He didn't turn around and make me leave with him. I wanted him to, even if it's wrong, Sally. I still wanted it so bad," I said slowly, hoping she understood.

"Come on, you big lug. Let's go for a walk. I saw some wild blooming salvia down the road, and I would like to look at it. Your presence is required. I think we have some stuff to talk about, don't you?" She took my hand and pulled on it gently as she helped me to my feet. I towered over her. I towered over most people. She looped her hand around my arm and guided me down the street.

"When did you know, Sally?" I asked sadly.

"What? That you weren't going to LA?" she squeezed my bicep gently. "I've known since you changed your departure date. You know, Hunter... I have grown very fond of you over the years. You're like another nephew to me, honey. But you are a rotten liar. Your poker face always gives you away."

"I didn't know what else to do, Sally. I don't want to be in his way. He's destined for greatness, I know it." The words tumbled out forcefully as if I could will them to be true. I wanted it so badly for Kris. He deserved everything he ever wanted, and he was talented enough to make it happen, I knew it.

"Perhaps," she mused. We walked slowly, meandering our way down the middle of the street as if we had no cares in the world. Appearances were deceiving. "Perhaps, not. What if he can only be great with you by his side? What if he has no drive, no ambition without you?"

"You don't believe that," I tried to laugh. It came out husky and sad. Already lonely without my other half.

"No, I don't suppose I do. But there is no way to know. He loves you with everything he has. If you don't go... I'm not sure he would ever understand, Hunter. Are you ready for that?" She stopped and reached up and took my face in her hands. "Please, do not tell me that you think you are a distraction to him. You deserve a life and a great education too, my love."

"I know... I will go to college... maybe. I think I would like to take a semester and figure some stuff out if Mom will let me. It's not that I will be in his way, Sally... It's that in the end, I know I will stop him from living the life he has always dreamed about. If I go, and I want to go, we will graduate, and he will come back here with me. This is where I want to be, but it is not where he needs to be, you know? He will grow to hate me, and I could never have that." I glanced away from her.

She took my hand and led me to a large gathering of purple flowers. Sally was always looking at or growing flowers. "You know what I detest, Hunter. Altruism. It usually back-fires and causes nothing but the opposite effect." She bent down and plucked a long purple bulb from the plant. "Salvia is one of my favorite plants. It contains so many properties within it. It's a plant of healing and cleansing, but when consumed, it can cause madness. It really is a lot like love, isn't it? So many different sides and ways to see things. Sometimes, Hunter, we need a little distance to see things clearly. Maybe that's what you need right now. But I know this. You two will be together, and you will grow old and be happy together until the day one of you dies. I have seen this, Hunter. You cannot change your destiny. Love is written in the stars."

"I want to believe that," I sighed.

"Come on. I'll sneak you a glass of wine. I'm sure they're drinking and crying too," she grinned.

I did think about it for two months, and with Sally's blessing, I finally made a decision. That decision would cause heartbreak for both of us. My heart has never recovered.

❧ 6 ❧

HUNTER (PRESENT DAY)

I should have stayed home.

But I let Sam talk me into meeting Crystal for a drink at Liberties Pub. She said she would meet us there and when we arrived, she was already feeling her oats.

"Lewis! Look who it is!" She exclaimed, pointing at us emphatically. "See! I do have friends. I knew they wouldn't leave me to the wolves again this week. Boys, what's your pleasure?"

Sam glanced over at me and smirked. "Well, this should be a laugh riot."

Before we could answer, Crystal, banged on the bar with her hand. "Redrum Ale! Right boys? Or are we gonna get wild tonight and join momma with a sip of gin." Her eyes widened. She looked like Betty Boop with curly red hair. I had not signed up for this. Something was definitely up. Crystal was a fun girl and all, but she was never a sloppy drunk.

"Lewis, honey. Get these two bitches a couple brews. They're too slow to answer for themselves," she raised her eyebrows and winked at us. "Lewis here has been telling me all about his trip to Iceland. Did you know Iceland is green and Greenland is ice? Did we learn that shit in school?"

Lewis poured our beers and shrugged at us. He mouthed, "Oh my God."

I agreed.

"Crystal, girlfriend... What is happening?" Sam laughed as he hugged her. "How fucking long have you been here?"

"Since I closed..." She cast her eyes away as she opened her mouth to say something, but she stopped herself. Well, either that or she forgot what she was going to say. "How long have I been here, Lewis?"

"When was Jesus born?" he snidely replied, shaking his head. Lewis loved Crystal, and I was sure he was now watering down her drinks. He took care of his friends, and as often as we all popped in, he took care of us.

"Lewis! I am not that old, and I have not been here that long, I don't think. I guess I should have eaten something. I didn't eat today. Lewis, can you get me some fried cheese curds with marinara?" she said, slowly working it out in her head. "Okay," she whispered incredibly loud. "I might have been here a little earlier than you. I've only had like two drinks."

Lewis held up four fingers behind her back.

"Hey, Lewis?" I asked quickly. "Can we get two tequila shots, please? I think we might need them." I nodded. He tried hard not to laugh, but a snicker escaped.

Crystal shot him a look. "Can I get one too, Lewis?"

"Uh... I don't think you need it, Crystal," Sam wrapped his arm around her and pulled her close. "This is so we can catch up to you, okay. You've been having too much fun without us."

"Well, that's my problem, isn't it?" she said seriously, which made us stare at her as if she had sprouted two heads. "I've not been having any fun at all. Everyone is busy with their life, and poor me is stuck being single and going out alone. Not you, Hunter... I know you're busy with search and rescue and can't come and play that often, but everyone else is happy and staying home, and I am stuck hanging out with Tad. I hate Tad."

"Everyone hates Tad. He's a dick." I grinned at her, trying to lighten her mood.

"Yes, he is. You know who else is a dick?" she asked, her mouth tightening and her chin wobbling as if she was trying to hold back her emotions. I don't know why... She just vomited them all over us.

"Who?" Sam asked. I wish he hadn't, but maybe it's good that he did.

"Larry is a dick," Crystal replied slowly. I glanced around to see if he was here. Larry was always here. He was like Norm or Cliff from Cheers. He sat at the same table every day.

Except for today. He was conspicuously absent, and that started to make everything make sense.

I scooted a stool over and sat in front of her, taking her hands in mine. "Why is Larry a dick, Crystal?"

She pouted. Of course, she did. Crystal was dramatic. She was the love child of Bette Davis and Dolly Parton, at least that's how we usually described her. "Larry stopped by yesterday and asked me if I was ever going to go out with him. I mean, we have gone out as friends a lot over the years..." She picked up her watered-down drink and took a sip.

"But he wants more?" Sam sympathized. He really was the best of us. He cared much more for everyone else than he ever did himself.

"Yeah... I told him that I didn't think it was a good idea." Her voice dripped with regret.

"Crystal... You have always wanted to. You're just scared

of settling down or committing to him. We all know it, honey. In the end, we all know you love him as much as he does you." I replied, rubbing the palm of her hand gently.

"Well, he said if that was the way I felt, then he was going to have to get over me. Tonight, I saw him walking down the street and entering Chez Tomlin Bistro with Annabeth Morrison. I hate that bitch." She frowned, setting her jaw tightly.

"No, you don't. Annabeth is fine, it's just that you're pissed off at Larry." Sam chided lovingly. You could tell he's been helping raise Lilly for the last couple of months. He had perfected *dad* voice.

"I think Larry is doing it to make you jealous. He has been mad about you for a decade. Crystal, you really need to think about this, my friend. You can't keep punishing yourself for something that happened..."

"Don't you dare, Hunter. I don't want to talk about that, right now. I just want to drink my troubles away, okay." She stared me down. I knew that meant the conversation was over. "And I know that I'm no good for Larry. I would only hurt him, and I don't want to do that boys. I want him to be happy... I do. I just... Things were safer when we could just flirt and have fun, you know."

"We do, honey," Sam bent down and kissed her on her cheek. She grinned at him.

"Okay, fellas. Why don't you take that shot and we go and boogie over at Rumors? Momma needs to dance her troubles away and maybe sweat out some of this gin. I'm fucking drunk!" She cackled, and Lewis brought her over a big glass of water.

"Hey, my sister. Drink this and hydrate if your gonna go dancing, okay?" he asked as he slid our shots over to us.

Sam and I picked them up and downed them quickly. We chugged our beer too and ordered another as Lewis brought

Crystal's fried curds to her. I have never seen her eat quite so ravenously. It was like a lion with a kill, Sam kept snickering, and Crystal slapped his hand as he tried to snag one.

We stumbled over to Rumors. Well, Crystal did anyway. Sam and I walked.

Johnny laughed when he saw us open the door. "Well, well, well! If it isn't three of my favorites. Hunter, good to see you, man. How's the station?" He gave me a fist bump.

"It's all good. We need to raise some money this spring as we've had a busy winter, but it's not been too bad." I smiled. Johnny was cool. He even stopped by every now and then and helped us around the station when he had time. He made a mean lasagna.

"Tell the boys hi from me. Sam... How's the husband? Is he still as hunky as ever?" He laughed.

"I pinch myself every day," Sam beamed.

"He's not his father, but he calls him daddy," Crystal teased. She was starting to sober up a little. Dancing would do her good. Johnny cackled with her, their laughs drowning out the disco music that was blaring from the speakers. "Is Tad here?"

"No. Thank God. You're safe, Crystal," he patted her on her head. "Have fun, guys."

"Come on, boys, let's boogie," Crystal grabbed my hand and pulled me towards the dance floor.

"I'll be there in a second. I need to go and say hi to Bruce." He waved at the bartender whose face had lit up as soon as he saw him.

We had a good night until we were about to leave. Sam just had to try once again to put Crystal on what he considered the right path for her. We were sitting at a table cooling off. My shirt was sticky with sweat, and Crystal smelled like a distillery.

"So, what are you gonna do, honey? Don't you think you

should talk to him and tell him how you feel?" he asked, leaning across the table.

"Why would I do that, Sam? You just don't really get it because you haven't had... Well, you just can't understand, I don't think. Hunter does." She turned to me. "You know what it is to love and to be solitary, don't you? You've been pining ever since he left, and you did it because you thought you were doing what was right."

"That's a totally different situation, Crystal," Sam said quickly, not wanting me to get all maudlin and shit. Crystal was right. He couldn't understand her point of view. We had a lot in common, even if our situations were vastly different. What happened to Crystal was... well, it was something that only a few people knew about. Love had not dealt her an easy hand when we were in high school, and she still carried the scars of her decision around like a giant piece of baggage. She could never forgive herself for what she had done, even if it had been her only choice at the time. She felt toxic when it came to love.

"I do understand, Crystal. But I also know that I regret that decision every day of my life and if I could take it back, or change it, in any way I could." I said sadly. "Don't make my mistakes. I wish I could find someone to love, I crave it, but..."

"There was only Kris. I know," she patted my arm gently. "Jesus Sam! You really know how to kill a good buzz." She laughed. "One more dance, and then we can get out of here, okay?"

She danced like there was no tomorrow. I dropped her off at her house and promised to pick her up in the morning. She was still not in any shape to drive, and she usually opened the store at 6 am.

I barely slept. All I could think about was him, and the choice I made that ended us for good.

✢ 7 ✢

KRIS (PRESENT DAY)

My trip was as arduous as I expected it to be. Getting to The Pleasant was as much a pain in the ass as I remembered. But it was also as beautiful as I remembered. As the helicopter sped over the lake, I was once again amazed by the size of it. The lake was even bigger than I remembered it. It took us twenty minutes to cross its placid waters, the sun beginning its descent behind the mountains and reflecting off the still clear water.

I saw the small town of Point Pleasant and breathed a small sigh of regret. Somewhere here was the one person I wished to see, but also hoped I wouldn't have to bump into. The way he hurt me... I don't think I would be able to see him and not relive the sadness of his absence. He chose that. He left me, and I have never even really known why.

Hopefully, he was fat and bald. I mean, he's in his twenties, so there was little chance of both being true. Maybe he moved away. I hope he did.

There were a few classmates I might track down, depending on how much work I really had to do. I mean, I was going to be here for a week, so eventually, I would have time to catch up. Of course, I would have to track them down if they were still here. When I moved away, I lost touch with everyone from here. They reminded me of Hunter and the relationship we had. Happy summers and cuddly winters of laughing and fun. They were the best times, and I hated to admit it but probably the best memories of my life so far. That was depressing.

The helicopter sped over the town and took me to the small landing platform on the edge of town. It didn't look like much had changed over the last decade. The buildings looked the same from the sky as I had remembered them. The twinkling lights from the park were easy to spot, and that was all I needed to get my orientation.

Time had been kind to The Pleasant, and it looked like it had been captured in its own time bubble. It hadn't really grown, of course; it sat between a lake and a mountain range, it didn't have much room to grow. But it did have charm. I had to admit that.

As I stepped off the small stairs with my bag, memories flooded into me. I walked toward the center of town and passed a baked goods shop that was new. However, it sat right between two stores from my youth. A bookstore and a small hobby shop that I used to frequent quite a bit. I loved that bookstore. They sold used and new books, and I always found something to open my imagination to worlds I had always dreamed of. I wonder if Mr. Delaney still owned it?

I passed the next block and slowed down. My aunt's house sat across the street. It hadn't changed, and there was even a small lamp turned on that sat in the front window. Fuck. I wished I could go and knock on that door and see her open it. But that was not reality. I was too late.

That's what should be inscribed on my fucking tombstone. 'He was too late,' had become something of a theme for me lately. My decisions or my inability to decide had bit me on the ass quite a bit over the last few years. I couldn't seem to find the desire to actually date. I went through the motions every now and then, but I never saw someone a second time. They just weren't the right person. I had given up any hope there because I was still stuck in that area of my life and probably always would be. I needed counseling. I wasn't interested in that either. I wasn't interested in much. Teaching was not my calling, I knew that even if it was my present and possible future. I would be a fool to throw that opportunity away, wouldn't I?

Fuck. I was already depressed, and these thoughts were making me spiral. I could feel darkness slowly creeping into my mind like a fog. If I dwelled on that right now, I wouldn't get through this, and I had to get through this. Aunt Sally deserved it. I deserved to relish in my memories and not beat myself up for what I didn't do. That was easier said than done, though.

I forced myself to walk away from her house. I had always loved it so much. It had been the place I was the happiest, I think. Making art, learning everything I know about photography from her, and most importantly, all the love and secrets Aunt Sally and I shared together in that house. It was also one of the prettiest houses on the street. What the fuck was I going to do with it? Maybe I could rent it? As soon as I had that thought, I regretted it. I couldn't do that, not to my memories. I would have to sell it eventually, and it would need some work done for that to happen.

But then there was the gallery and her attached studio in the middle of town. What the hell would I do with that? Closing it would make me feel I was erasing her and her work from the community she loved, but I couldn't run it. My life was not here, and I had no desire to make this place home. I never had. That's what broke my heart in the end, I had always believed.

"Oh shit," I laughed as I passed by Margie's Coffee Shop. It used to be called The Court Square coffee Shop, but Crystal's mom changed the name when we were in high school. I had good memories of that place and Crystal. I wonder if she was still in town. It was closed, so I couldn't ask Margie if she even still owned it.

I passed by and walked to the address I had been given by the lawyer. It was a cute cottage with a picture window. I wonder if there was where Mrs. Markle always lived? It really was adorable and exactly what you expected a bed and breakfast in this town to look like. A small wooden sign sat in the yard announcing 'The Point Pleasant Bed & Breakfast.' I walked up the small set of stairs and onto her little porch and knocked on the door.

I wonder if she'll remember me? I wondered.

The door opened, and my old English teacher stood there with a wide smile upon her face. Her eyes twinkled as she looked at me. I smiled back.

"Mrs. Markle, it's really great to see you again," I giggled. All of a sudden, I was seventeen years old again and worried she wouldn't like my book report.

"Kris! Oh my goodness, child. Look at you... You have become a man," she cooed, pulling her cardigan tight against her small frame. "I just can't believe it. I was beginning to wonder if I would ever see you again." She took a step backward and gestured for me to enter.

"This house is adorable. I love the gingerbread trim around the roof. It's beautiful." I stepped through, and she shut the door behind me before patting me on the back.

"Thank you, Kris. It's always been my safe place, and after I retired and Mr.Markle passed away, well, it got a little lonely. So, I started a new business. I love it. Come on in, honey. I started dinner, and it will be ready soon. I bet you're hungry after that trip in from Los Angeles," she supposed correctly.

I sat my bag down by the door. "I am famished, Mrs. Markle. This trip happened so fast, I barely had time to eat a bagel before I boarded the flight." I was tired, but the thought of eating was making my mouth salivate. I had so much tension about coming back here that I had forgotten about my actual needs until she mentioned it. Whatever she was cooking smelled delicious.

"I'm sure, Kris. I am so sorry about Sally. She was a dear friend and an amazing artist. That painting at the top of the stairs is one of hers. You'll see it when I show you your room," she fluttered. Mrs. Markle was always an energetic teacher, and aging hadn't seemed to slow her down. "Oh shit! Hold on, Kris. I need to take the lasagna out of the oven and let it sit for a few minutes. I'll be right back."

She went around the corner and disappeared from view. I walked around the far side of the couch and sat down. Oh God... Sitting somewhere soft felt like a luxury after the day I had. Whoever created airplane seats was a sadist and hated human beings, I was sure of that. My ass was sore from all of the sitting.

"Kris, do you want me to show you up to your room before dinner? I can take you up as soon as I get this garlic bread back in the oven. I wasn't sure if you ate meat anymore, so I made veggie lasagna. I hope that's okay," she exclaimed loudly from the kitchen. I could hear her banging something. "Goddammit! Oops! Sorry, Kris."

I laughed. "Oh, don't mind me, Mrs. Markle. I like a good curse word."

Her laughter filled the kitchen and soothed me in some way. She was always a motherly type of teacher and one of my favorites. She always made her classes fun and exciting. I was a pale imitation of her. Even I might fall asleep in my art history class. It was boring.

"Never trust a person who doesn't cuss. That's what my husband believed. So, Harry said you're a teacher now? I couldn't believe it. I always thought you would be an artist like Sally. You were so talented." She walked back around the corner and grinned at me. "It really is good to see you, Kris. You were always one of my brightest students. You had so many plans in that head of yours. So what made you decide to become a teacher?"

"I'm not sure I really have a good answer. I am a professor at West Beverly University in the art department. I teach photography and art history. I don't think that I am anywhere as good of a teacher as you, though. I just got tired of the grind of being a poor artist and wanted a steady paycheck. I'm not sure it's a good fit if I'm being honest. Did you always know you wanted to be a teacher?" I asked, curious about her answer.

"Oh, God, no! I had wanted to be a writer, but I realized during college that even though it was a passion of mine, I didn't really have the talent for it. So, I got a degree in educa- tion. That first few years of teaching were a nightmare. I fumbled through most of it, but then something clicked within me. I started enjoying it and realized that my joy was contagious to the kids. That's when I knew that teaching was a calling for me. As a writer, I was great at grammar but horrible at the plot. As a teacher, I became the writer I had always wanted to be. You kids were my characters, and the plot was Shakespeare and Jane Austen. I think the novel of my life is an exciting adventure, and these last few chapters are a gift to me."

I stared at her. The passion with which she spoke sent warmth through me. "I was just offered a chance for a tenured position at the college. I am trying to decide what it is I want, I guess. If I take it, my art career is over. To have a career as an artist, I can't rely on teaching as security. I guess you can say I am at the crux in my own story." I shrugged, feeling a little boastful, even mentioning it. But I wouldn't mind the advice of someone I had always admired.

"Bullshit, honey. You're still in the early chapters," she giggled. "I can tell you this, though. Follow your passion and your heart, not your mind. The heart will never lead you down the wrong path if you listen closely. The mind is a trickier beast, Kris. It's filled with fear and anger and can steer you away from the path you are meant to be on. Use it wisely, and it's a friend. follow it blindly, and your life will be filled with regrets."

"My heart hasn't been an excellent guide so far, Mrs. Markle," I said sadly.

"Kris? Are you sure it's your heart you've been listening to?" she walked over and touched me on the arm. "Come on, honey. Let's show you your room. I'm sure you would like to freshen up a little before dinner. Grab your bag."

I followed her up the stairs, and she showed me Aunt Sally's painting. It was as striking and beautiful as all of her work. Her photos were a stark contrast to her painting, and I always found that dichotomy interesting about her work. Her photos had a calmness to them that made you feel at ease. But her paintings were wild and erratic as if she spilled passion on the canvas. She had succeeded in the art world with both of her chosen mediums, a feat that many artists never accomplished.

Mrs. Markle left me in my room after showing me what I needed to know. The room was small but lovely and had its own private bathroom, which I was happy about. I had always been a thin person. I tried to go to the gym and bulk up, I ate protein and did everything my trainer told me, but I was still a bean pole, as my father always teased. I hated having to walk around shirtless, so I was glad I had access to a shower in my room.

After I brushed my teeth and put away my clothes, I went downstairs and joined Mrs. Markle for the most delicious vegetable lasagna I had ever eaten. She opened a bottle of wine, and the two of us picked up our glasses and toasted each other when we were finally done eating.

"Do any of your friends know that you're here?" she raised her right eyebrow at me, knowingly.

"I... uh... I haven't been good at staying in touch with people. When... Well, what happened... happened, I just lost touch with everyone." I wrinkled my nose unhappily. Telling the truth like that made me feel like an asshole. "I'm not sure they would want to see me. I thought about trying to find Crystal."

"Well, that won't be hard, Kris. She's at Margie's every day. She owns and runs it now," Mrs. Markle laughed.

"Really? That's great." I smiled at her. The thought of Crystal running the coffee shop she used to hate made me smile. I guess we have all changed.

"Most everyone is still here, honey. Danny, Wally, and Sam are still around. I guess you heard about Dylan?" she leaned onto the table, a smirk on her face.

"No... Oh my God... is he okay?" I said, worried. He was always a sweetie. Even though he was a year behind me, we had been friends. All of us gay boys and Crystal were tight back then.

"Honey, Okay? He is marrying a prince," she exclaimed. "He's fucking royalty."

My mouth hit the floor. Things really had changed around here.

"But, I don't think they are who you really want to know about, are they?" she surmised shrewdly.

"No... I think that's it, Mrs. Markle," I replied, my voice a little chilly. She shook her head at me as if she was disappointed.

"You know he's been miserable all these years, don't you?" she said quietly. "He has a lot of regrets."

"Don't we all?" I answered. "I am beat, Mrs. Markle. This has been a long day, and I can't even imagine what tomorrow is going to be like. Would you mind if I went to bed? Do you need help with the dishes or anything?" I asked, ending the conversation before it went down the road I didn't want it to.

"No, Kris, I have this. It's what I do now. You go upstairs and go to bed. It really has been lovely getting to sit down and catch up, though. You have a good night's sleep." She stood up and picked up our plates. I drank my last sip of wine and walked to the door.

"Good night, Mrs. Markle," I turned and smiled at her.

"Pleasant dreams, Kris," she grinned back.

I was asleep before my head hit the pillow.

🪝 8 🪝

HUNTER (PRESENT DAY)

It's nice to have a few days off. The guys at the station were starting to get on my nerves. We badly need to have a fundraiser of some kind, but the person who usually did it retired in the fall, right before our busiest season. None of the guys want to pick up the slack, which means it's probably going to fall to me. I would be shit at organizing a bake sale.

Gary was a great chief, and we haven't actually replaced him. I was the second in command, so I've been trying to keep things on the up and up, but damn those guys can be a handful. Sometimes I feel like the only way to get them to wash the damn dishes is to act like a drill sergeant. I never wanted to be in charge, it's not my personality. I'd rather go on a hike, or downhill with Danny when he's around, not bark orders all day at those idiots.

Okay, so I do like them. I just don't really enjoy being in charge of them. Gary is a hard man to replace. Last year he and his wife organized a spring dance for the town and tourists to go to. We made bank on ticket sales alone, and the wine and finger foods were donated by the Point Pleasant

Winery, so it was all profit. When you add on the silent auction and *Win a Dinner with a Fireman*, we were flush for the year.

That's run out, and we are going to be in a world of hurt, soon if I don't figure something out. The mayor has reminded me about our financial woes for the last couple of months. How the hell do you organize anything during your busiest time of the year?

Sally's lawyer called me today, and I have to meet someone at her house this afternoon to give them the keys to her place. That's gonna suck balls. She gave me some of her most beautiful pieces of art that I had always admired and all the photos of us that I had always cherished. It wasn't hard to be with her through this, I mean, yes, it was hard to watch someone you love going through everything she did, but it was where I wanted to be. She had always been there for me too, and these last nine years, we had grown close. She became my best friend when Kris and I ended. I assume that's' why he didn't come around if he knew. We didn't talk about him. She knew that chapter of my life had to be closed, even if she also knew I had never moved on. Sally was like that. She didn't meddle.

I left the little house I purchased last year and walked down towards the court square. I needed inspiration today. I needed a friend, and that meant only a handful of people. Danny had just got back in town, and I didn't want to bother him. I was sure he was tired after flying back from LA like a star. Blake had him fly private, he had moved up in the world a lot like Dylan... And here I was left in The Pleasant... Yeah, it was going to be a dark day.

I sat in the park for a while, the chirps of the birds soothed my tired soul. The spring flowers were shooting up out of the ground, and a few had opened just to test the weather. They were a part of The Pleasant too and knew the drill. The weather could change at a moment's notice. I've heard visitors use that joke about where they live, and I just laughed. Here in The Pleasant, it wasn't a joke. It was facts.

I waved at a few passersby that I've known since childhood. I was glad they didn't come to shoot the shit today because I wasn't really in the mood. Maybe Crystal would want to go out again tonight, I was sure I could use the company and a drink later.

What asshole bought Sally's place? I was sure that it had to be the case because the Boltons had already been here, and it wasn't them. Knowing Sally, she might have even donated the building to one of her charities. Honestly, there was no telling what she had done. She had always been a wild card that you could never read. Just another reason I loved her.

I got up off the hard, wooden bench and jogged across the street to Margie's. I could use a coffee and might as well talk to Crystal. I needed the company, and she was one of the best people to talk to when you needed advice. I bet she was hurting today. When I picked her up and dropped her off this morning, she was comatose.

I understood why she tied one on last night. It's hard to let go and love when you don't feel worthy, and Crystal and I were birds of a feather when it came to matters of the heart. I opened the door and caught her leaning against the counter with her eyes closed.

She didn't move. Holy shit! She was sound asleep. It was about two in the afternoon, and here she was, passed out, sleeping while standing up. It was a talent.

I creep-walked slowly up to her until I was on the other side of the counter. I slowly leaned in until my face was only a few inches from hers. I almost stopped myself. This was a complete asshat move, but I couldn't let this opportunity pass me by, it was too awesome to allow good judgment to get the better of me.

"Coffee, bitch!" I hollered, a wide grin spreading across my face.

Her eyes flew open, and without missing a beat, her hand plummeted through the air towards my face. I barely got out of the way in time. She lost her balance and quickly deposited herself onto the floor behind the counter. I fell onto the floor too, laughing, barely able to breathe. Yeah, it was worth it.

"You son of a bitch! You scared the fucking shit out of me!" she thundered as she slowly stood up. I looked up at her, a wide grin spread across my face as I tried to contain my glee. "Hunter Bradley, I would kick your ass if I didn't have to walk around this counter. I can't believe you did that!"

I crawled off the floor and stood up in front of her. "I can't believe you were napping on the job. Seriously, how did you even do that?" I smirked, trying to contain my laughter. She was not in the mood, and I should have expected that. Still... It was completely worth it.

"I just shut my eyes for a minute, I swear." She looked up at the cuckoo clock on the wall, and her eyes widened. "Holy shit! It's two? I wonder how many customers came in and saw me and just left? I'm not sure, Hunter, but I think I've been asleep a couple of hours," she said incredulously. "Fuck..."

"I'm sorry, Crystal. I know you had a long day, but you can't really blame me..." I tried to look apologetic, even if I would have done it again.

"Shit... I would have done it too. I was so fucking tired. I can't believe I actually opened this place. Hey, at least my hangover is gone. Now I'm just tired. How are you feeling, honey? I'm sorry that I... well, you know. I was fucking drunk. I still have to go get my car. Maybe you'll want to walk over with me. You know, hair of the dog and all." She winked.

"Yeah. I'll come back over at six and help you close, and then we can go unwind. I will definitely need to. Sally's lawyer called me today and told me that I have to meet the new

owner and show them around, you know, give them the keys and everything. I just think it sucks that all of her stuff is still in there. It bothers me that some stranger is going to have all her things that she didn't bequeath to someone. I mean, the Bolton's got what they wanted and what she had left to them in her will, and I took the things she wanted me to have before she passed away. I helped her send all of the art that she donated to the different museums and galleries, but the rest of it... I mean there's still a lot of her work in that house. Shit, her studio and gallery are filled with stuff still... I just..."

I sat down on the stool and buried my head in my hands, trying to stop myself from getting emotional. Crystal was a safe place, and I had already cried on her shoulder numerous times over Sally's death. I was just afraid if I opened that door on today of all days, I wouldn't be able to close it. I squeezed my eyes tight.

"She loved you so much, Hunter." Crystal ran her fingers through my hair. "Yep! I think we will definitely need a drink tonight. What time are you supposed to go over there?"

"In a couple hours. If losing someone hurts this much, Crystal... I think we both made the right choices, don't you?" I inhaled slowly. My neck felt like a cold, clammy towel had wrapped around it.

"I think you know where I stand, honey. Were you coming here just to see me, or do you want momma to make you a coffee?" she leaned in and kissed my forehead.

"Please? I didn't sleep much either, you know," I laughed gently.

"How bad was I last night?" she wrinkled her nose in disgust. "Was I a total bitch?"

I raised my head and puckered my lips together. "You were a little wild but not a total bitch. For the most part, it was fun. Are you okay?"

She ran her hands through her disheveled hair. "Describe

okay. I'm annoyed at how hurt I was at seeing him with someone else. It's not like it's the first time, even. Come on, Larry and I have had this dance before. This time it just felt more real, you know, like this is actually the end. He deserves better than me, and we all know it." She turned around and grabbed a cup from the shelf.

"That is not true, my love. Anyone would be lucky to have you in their life, Crystal. Look at all of us. You've been our angel for years." I stood up and stretched, my back popping back into place.

"Do you gotta go? Stay here and be miserable with me," she pleaded as she added some coffee to her press.

"Just got to use the bathroom, girlfriend. You're stuck with me for a little. Shit, I think you need me to stay awake," I laughed as I headed down the small hall to the bathroom.

I looked at myself in the mirror when I was done. I knew how handsome I was, but it didn't really matter to me. I was a mess on the inside. It didn't matter how pretty my outside was when my inside was so ugly.

I washed my hands and walked out of the door. I heard someone else in the shop, and when I walked back into the main room, I almost passed out.

Kris was standing at the counter.

❧ 9 ❧

KRIS (PRESENT DAY)

Mrs. Markle made a huge breakfast. I had no idea when she baked all the fresh pastries and croissants, but they were piping hot and delicious. So was the omelet. Bless her. I think I would move in with her if she was in LA. I could quickly get used to someone taking care of me like that again.

I had a meeting with the lawyer at twelve, and I said my goodbyes to sweet Mrs. Markle and headed to walk around town for a bit before I went to his office. I had been right in my earlier estimation about The Pleasant. It had not changed one iota. Some businesses had changed names, and there were a few restaurants I didn't remember, but for the most part, it was still The Pleasant I remembered.

My walking tour brought back a lot of memories. Most of them were tinged with pain because Hunter was a part of almost all of them. I decided to head over to the bookstore since it was right around the corner from Mr. Bennarde's office.

The Point Pleasant bookstore had been a saving grace for me. Mr. Delaney stocked it with all the bestsellers, but my

favorite thing was to comb through the used book section. I had found some gems hidden away on those shelves, and I found myself returning to them as if they were old friends on occasion. Hell, I still had most of the books I bought here. I was a minimalist in most aspects of my life, but books were something I could never let go of. They were too important to me, and getting rid of a book I loved was like losing someone I cared about.

I stood in front of the small window and laughed. There, on the display, was the same Shakespeare tome that had always fascinated me. It was a large leather-bound monstrosity that was about as big as a child. It sat in the window, luring customers inside, promising an experience of awe and inspiration if you would just walk through the door. I had stared at that book for years, wondering how heavy it had to be and how anyone could ever read it. The sheer monstrosity of it was frightening, but what secrets did it hold between its pages. Mr. Delaney never let anyone touch it. He told me once that it had never even been opened and was in mint condition. It sat upon a stand that had wheels so he could put it in the safe room every night.

I opened the door and walked inside. I grinned at how much the store was still the same as from my childhood. I perused the shelves as I walked towards the desk that was overcrowded with stacked books, just as always. Mr. Delaney was usually perched behind them, reading one of his treasures.

I stopped in front of the desk. I don't know why I felt so shy. It had been too many years. There was no way he would remember me, would he?

"Mr. Delaney?" I asked timidly, feeling like that fourteen-year-old kid who had first come in here.

A young man peered over the books, his bright blue eyes were piercing and sharp through his large black glasses. His short hair stood up in the front, and he smiled at me. He looked like someone who wore his nerdiness as a badge. He was very cute in a, 'I really don't care what you think,' way.

"Hi," he grinned, looking me up and down. I felt like a piece of meat. "Mr. Delaney doesn't come into the store much anymore. I bet you used to live here and are back for a visit, huh? I'm just guessing because I don't recognize you, and Mr. Delaney hasn't been coming in much for the last few years."

"Oh... Yeah, you guessed it. How is he doing?" I asked, worried that this titan from my childhood had gotten ill. After Aunt Sally, it wouldn't surprise me. My emotions were on edge from being back here, and it seemed like they were just going to get worse.

"He's great. I bet he's out on the golf course right now. That's how he likes to spend his time when it's nice, and we are having a pretty great start to spring right now. Hi there." He stuck his hand out and offered it to me. I shook it. "I'm Hart, and I guess I manage the store now. I'm the only full-time employee anyway. We have a high school girl who works on Saturdays for us. Where did you come in from?" He stared at me with a huge lopsided grin on his face. He really was adorable, and I'm guessing older than he looks. I assumed he was a high school kid.

"Hi there, it's nice to meet you, Hart. I'm... uh, Kris Bolton, and I'm visiting from Los Angeles." I smiled back at him. His grin really was infectious.

"Bolton? Are you kin to Sally?" I nodded. "I am so sorry for your loss. She was a great lady. I used to bring her books up to her house to read. Mr. Delaney said she was the kind of lady whose brain was always hungry for more. He really admired her. I did too, hell, I guess the whole town did. How long are you in for?" He walked around the desk and leaned against the shelf in front of me.

He was shorter than me. I guess he might have been about five-eight, but he was just as skinny as me. He had a very handsome round face and eyes that were hard to look away from. They were a deep blue and pulled you in.

"Just for the week. I'm on spring break, right now," I admitted.

"Are you in college? How do we not know each other? What year did you graduate?" he crossed his arms and peered deeply into my eyes, his lips tightening as he studied me.

"I'm actually a college professor, Hart," I laughed. "I graduated ten years ago this May. I guess you could say this is my homecoming. I haven't been back here since I moved away. My parents moved to Seattle."

"Oh shit! You are Sally's nephew, the photographer. She talked about you a lot. Wow! She was, like, really proud of you. She said you had the golden eye and could see something in the ordinary that no one else could see. She even showed me a few of your pieces of artwork she had framed in her house." He bounced on the balls of his feet when he talked. It was kind of adorable.

"How old are you, Hart?" I asked, feeling a little like an old letch for wondering. He just looked so young.

"Oh, I'm twenty-two. I just graduated from college last year and moved back when I finished. I worked here when I was in high school and ever summer between semesters. I always knew this was my destiny. This store is everything to me and always has been. We still do the Saturday morning reading for the kids and everything. I never missed one when I was growing up." He walked back behind the desk and grabbed a flyer. "Stop by this weekend. I bet its exactly like you remember. Hey? Do you want me to call Mr. Delaney for you? He might stop by to read for the kids this Saturday. It's about the only time he really comes in anymore. He's enjoying being retired, but I bet he would love to see you."

"No need to call him, Hart. I will have my hands full this week with Aunt Sally's estate, but I may try to stop by on Saturday. That would be a nice bookend to my trip, I think. Anyway, I won't keep you. I'm sure you have stuff to do, but it was very nice to talk to you." I smiled at him before I turned and walked back to the door.

"Hey, Hart? Have you ever touched that Shakespeare book?" I asked curiously.

"Are you kidding me? Mr. Delaney would skin me alive if my finger ever touched the leather. But I wheel it into its special room every day. It's heavy as fuck." He laughed loudly. "I threw my back out once."

"That's what I've always wondered. How could anyone read it?" I shook my head as my hand reached for the door.

"There are more things in Heaven and Earth Horatio, than are dreamt of in your philosophy," He quoted proudly. That was the same line that Mr. Delaney always said. I turned around and laughed loudly.

"That's what Mr. Delaney always said. I think this store is in the right hands, Hart," I said as I opened the door and stepped back outside.

Damn.

Things change, but somehow, even with the differences, this perfect place from my childhood still felt the same. Even if looking at Hart made me feel old for some reason. If I had the time, I might try to stop by on Saturday to see the old owner and hear him read to the children. It was something that felt like comfort in a week that I knew was going to feel turbulent.

I walked down the street and turned the corner and saw my destination in front of me. Mr. Bennarde's office was a small brick building that used to be something else, I just couldn't remember what it once was. I remember going in there with my mother once... What the fuck was it?

I opened the door and failed to have the epiphany I was hoping for. An incredibly small waiting room with a couch, two chairs, and a TV sat on top of an incredibly dilapidated rug that was threadbare at best. There was a small reception window, but nobody was behind it, so I waited in one of the chairs. Some soap opera played on the TV.

After a few minutes, a small rotund woman ambled in from outside and opened the door to the inner offices and sat behind the desk. I took a breath and walked over and stood in front of her.

She glanced up at me and held up a finger before I could speak. She fiddled with her computer, and I noticed that she had on fake eyelashes that were so massive it looked like she was auditioning for a spot on Rupaul's Drag Race. After what felt like an eternity of standing and waiting, she cleared her throat and smiled at me.

"How can I help you, sweetheart?" she asked in a heavy southern accent. "Oh! Are you Sally's nephew, honey?"

I nodded, and before I could speak, she shot up out of her chair.

"Well, shit! Harry will have my ass, making you wait out here. I had to go across the street to smoke my cigarette because Harry yells at me if he sees me. He's been trying to get me to quit forever, but you know how it is. If I quit smoking, I might slap the son of a bitch!" She cackled. "They keep me calm, honey, even if they are bad for me. I've always figured smoking is better than being put in San Quintin if you catch my drift. I would hate to kill someone!" She cackled again.

I picked my jaw up off the floor and grinned stupidly back at her. She had flummoxed me.

"Harry! Mr. Bolton is here!" she screamed down the hallway behind her.

The bald head of a very old man peeked around the doorframe. "Kris? My how you have grown up, young man. Send him back, Bree. Would you like something to drink, Kris? Coffee or a soda?"

"Or perhaps a water, honey?" The receptionist, whose name I know knew was Bree asked me his eyelashes fluttering delicately.

"I'll take a Coke if you have it?" I asked. I hadn't really drunk soda in a long time, but for some reason, maybe it was just being back here, made me crave one at the mention of it.

"What kind do you want?" she asked, making my head jumble as I tried to figure out what she meant. "What kind of coke?"

"Uh... normal, I guess," I said, trying to understand what she meant.

"Noooooo! I meant what kind of coke? Like do you want a Sprite or a Dr. Pepper? Maybe a diet?"

"Just a Coke, I guess," I managed.

"Oh, Jesus, Bree! You are not in the south anymore! A Coke is a goddamned Coke! A Sprite is a fucking Sprite! Forgive her, Kris. Where she's from all sodas are cokes. It took me forever to figure that out. Come on back!" Mr. Bennarde bellowed from the doorway.

This was weird. The whole office felt like a Fellini movie. I kept expecting a camera crew to come out and tell me I was being punk'd, but that was in the past, too, just like my life here. Aunt Sally would have loved this madness. I can see why this was the lawyer she chose.

Bree opened the door. "Go on back, honey, and tell that asshole I might shake his coke up and spray his ass with it." She snickered under her breath. "Go on. I'll bring them in a minute." She mimed having a cigarette.

I walked through the door and down the old wood-paneled walls when it hit me. This used to be a dentist's office when I was a kid. I remembered walking down this hallway when Mom brought me with her one day. Strange that the memory rushed in like that. I turned and entered into Harry Bennarde's office. He stood in front of his desk.

Mr. Bennarde was an incredibly short and thin man with an even thinner pencil mustache. Yep! He was straight from a Fellini movie... He grinned at me and stuck out his hand.

"Mr. Bolton, do you mind if I call you Kris? I'm not one of those men that craves formality. Please call me Harry, all of my friends and clients do. Your aunt used to love to sing that old song to me whenever she would walk into the office. You know? I'm Just Wild About Harry?" I shook my head. He talked fast, and I barely understood most of the words flying from his mouth.

"No matter, young man. That was well before your time, I suppose. One of the issues about getting older Kris is people you meet stop getting your cultural references. I still can't figure out what a fucking Kardashian is..." He roared with laughter. "Okay, have a seat there. This won't take long at all, Kris. I know you must have a few questions, but let's get to the particulars so you can go about your visit home."

He walked around his desk and sat in his large leather chair. I had to stop my self from laughing. I dug my fingernails into the palms of my hands to stop the sniggering from happening. He looked like a very old child in that large chair.

"I spoke to your parents while they were here. Sally left them a few things, and we had to go and get them from the house. She also let them take any of her possessions that they chose, except for her art. She said that would be up to you. The pieces that she chose for the various galleries and museums have already been shipped to them before her death. She was a stickler for how they were to be handled and had someone she trusted to take care of it all." He leaned onto his desk and rested his chin in his hands as he stared at me. He had sad eyes that looked as if he had been crying or had bad seasonal allergies. But they were kind. I could see why Aunt Sally chose him.

"Sally's caretaker has the keys to the house, studio, and the gallery in his possession. He will meet you in front of the house at four today if that's okay with you? He took care of Sally in her decline, but they had been good friends for years. I thought he was her nephew for quite some time, actually. He was a blessing to her and took her to all of her doctor appointments and stayed with her for the last couple of months when she couldn't take care of herself. He's a fine boy, and I think you'll get along great. Really, Kris, all I need from you is your signature on these documents, and all will be in order. Her property will belong to you to do with as you wish."

He handed me the pen, and I signed my name wherever he pointed his finger. I was numb. This is what had become of her, these papers for me to sign and her belongings became mine. It didn't seem fair. I would rather have her laughing at this insanity with me.

He sat back and smiled at me. "It doesn't seem fair, does it? That this is what it comes to. But, she spoke of you often, Kris, and this was her wishes."

"Yeah..." I said quietly. "It's...I... I don't know what to say or... even feel right now, honestly. I'm just dazed, I guess. It's all a little too much to take in." I could feel the knot in my throat, threatening to rise up. The sweat on the back of my neck meant that my emotional state was getting chaotic, and I really wanted to run the fuck out of here and not look back.

"Do you know what you're going to do yet. Kris? With the property, I mean. Sally's gallery meant quite a bit to this town."

I shook my head in acknowledgment. "I know... Honestly, I'm not sure what she was thinking. My life is in LA, and I have no idea what I'm supposed to do. I can't imagine selling

Sally's place or her studio, and I know she would haunt me if I even thought about the gallery, but I just don't know right now."

"Well, young man..." He raised his eyebrows at me. They were as thin as his mustache. "You will figure it out, I suppose. If I can be of any help, please let me know." He opened a drawer in his desk. "I have two letters for you from your aunt. She left me with very detailed instructions, as she knew that this would be a hard decision for you to make. I am to give you the one that matches your decision."

Once again, I pulled my jaw off the floor. Sally always knew, somehow.

He held up the envelope in his right hand with a small drawing that Sally doodled on it. "This one is for you if you decide to stay in Point Pleasant." He held up the one in his left hand without a doodle. "This one is if you decide to return to LA and sell the property. Let me know when you make your decision, Kris. I'm sorry I can't give you the letters until you decide. She left very strict instructions, and I cannot go against her wishes."

I stood up slowly. "I understand. Is that it, Mr. Bennarde? I mean, Harry..." I sounded like a zombie. She knew that I wouldn't know what to do, so she gave me the two options I should consider. In the end, which would she think was truly best for me?

"Yes, Kris. I bet that Bree has a coke out there waiting for you. I'm sure she just got back from her sneaky cigarette break. Please let me know if I can be of any help. Sally's caretaker will meet you at four in front of the house. I know this is difficult, Kris. Please don't be afraid to reach out if you need me." He held out his hand, and I shook it limply. I was in shock. Sally always had a way of flooring me when I least expected it, and this one was a doozy.

I walked out of the office in a daze, and Bree stood there,

grinning at me with a can of Coke held in her hand. "Here you go, honey. I hope it was what you wanted."

I took it and thanked her before I walked out into The Pleasant's sunny afternoon. I was about to open it to take a drink when I realized that this wasn't what I wanted. I needed coffee. More than that, I needed a friend, and there was one that I hoped might be available to chat.

I walked as fast as my frazzled body would allow until I stood in front of Margie's Coffee Shop. I peered through the glass and saw my old friend with her wild curly red hair behind the counter, making something in one of the machines. I took a deep breath and prepared myself for what might be a chilly reception. I would deserve it. But I hoped she would forgive me because I really felt lost, and Crystal had always been a beacon of stability for us if not for herself. Maybe she had finally found her own peace. I hoped so, well... I was about to find out.

I opened the door and walked slowly up to the counter.

"Just a second, okay?" she said as she fussed about with whatever she was doing.

"Sure, Red," I said, using the nickname I had always called her.

I saw her shoulders stiffen, and she slowly turned around, her mouth agape. "Holy shit..." she muttered.

Okay, so this wasn't going the way I hoped.

"Kris? Holy shit... You really have bad timing, don't you?" She stared at me. "Holy shit! Is it really you?" she beamed at me.

"It's really me," I smiled back.

"Oh... Sally... I'm really sorry, Kris, I... Well, you know how much we all adored her. Still, it's... Well, it's been a long time," she tilted her head as if she were studying me, trying to decide what to do next.

"Yeah... Sorry. I've been a bit of an ass, I guess." I shrugged.

"You look good, honey. Becoming a man looks hot on you," Crystal winked, sticking her tongue out. I giggled.

"Holy shit," a deep voice caught me unawares. I would recognize that voice for as long as I could remember my own name. I turned towards it, and he stood there.

He wasn't fat. Fuck... He was even more gorgeous than the last time I had seen him. He was a man... A very manly, sexy man with bulging muscles and eyes that looked right into your soul.

"Hi, Hunter," I managed before feeling the floor hit my face.

10

KRIS (THE PAST)

Hunter had called and told me that he was delaying his trip again. It was the second time. I mean, I get it, I do. He's a little scared of the big city and leaving everything he loved behind, but right now, I felt as if he were leaving me behind.

It was fucking depressing. This wasn't how I had planned for LA to be. I had expected that he would be following directly behind me, and we would be experiencing all of these amazing things together. I really wanted to show him the LA County Museum of Art. It was breathtaking, and Aunt Sally had a piece on display in their permanent collection of photography. I couldn't wait to show it to Hunter. A piece of The Pleasant, right here in LA.

If only he would come.

'One month,' he said. One month was a long time.

I had been in LA for two months, and it had been fucking fantastic! It was everything that I had hoped it would be. The classes were solid, and college life was one fun night after another. Well, at first it sucked, if I'm honest. All I did was pine away for Hunter. I sat in my dorm room until one of the girls in my life drawing class made me go to a party with her. After that, I tried to enjoy myself as much as possible. I still missed Hunter terribly, but he wasn't here, and I was. He was probably hanging out with his boys and having fun. He really didn't say much when we talked, which was almost daily, when he answered his fucking phone. Frustrating as it was, I still called him a couple times a day until he picked up. He was working with his Uncle on his farm, and I hoped he was saving his money to make the move.

But I didn't know that for sure. Right now, the only thing I knew for sure was I was getting a B in art history, and I wouldn't be complete until he arrived to be with me. Hunter would love college as much as me, I knew it. He was lucky they allowed him to delay his acceptance by a semester. What really ticked me off about that is he did it without telling me. I didn't know until I arrived in LA. He should have told me. Even if he didn't want to hold me back, and I get that, I do, but I didn't like being lied to, even if the lie was an omission of the truth. We deserved more in our relationship.

Hunter and I were meant to be together. Aunt Sally had told me that, and she had an uncanny knack for knowing the future. Dad always said she was the family seer. He joked, but there was also a reverence to it. He believed whatever his sister told him without questioning it. As did I.

I talked to Aunt Sally weekly. We discussed the artists I was learning about and the work that made them special. I couldn't wait until we got to the contemporary art history class. She knew a lot of those people. They were her peers.

The professor of my life drawing class knew Aunt Sally. He was a fan of her work, and they had known each other many years ago when they were both starting out in the art world. Sally succeeded, and my professor started teaching after a few years. Sally said he was sweet but had nothing to say that hadn't already been said better by someone else. That was the way of the art world. It was all about your vision and how you could bring something new to something already done. I had met a screenwriter who told me that there were only really five stories to be told, and every movie ever made would fall easily into one of those categories, following a plot already written. That was depressing. Life was depressing and would be until Hunter came home to me. I was his home, and he was mine, even if he was scared of it for some reason.

I had made a few cool friends. They weren't as great as my friends back in The Pleasant, I mean, Crystal and Danny were hard to beat. They were having fun in college too. We stayed in touch via texts and Facebook. They were enjoying college more than me but kept telling me that Hunter was going to show up. I wanted to believe them.

My best friend here was this geeky guy named Lil' Joe. At least, that's what he wanted to be called. He was interesting, if not a bit weird. I think he had a crush on me, but that wasn't happening, of course. But he was fun, and I enjoyed spending time with him, even if I did feel like he wanted more from me. He made me feel happy, at least, and that was something I needed.

What I really needed was Hunter.

One month. I could wait for one month, couldn't I?

11

HUNTER (PRESENT DAY)

"Kris!" Crystal screamed as I stood there, dumbly. My feet felt glued to the floor as the man I loved slumped to the floor, narrowly missing his head on the side of a table. My body tingled as if it had fallen asleep, every nerve stood on edge as I watched Crystal run around the counter.

How was he here? Why the fuck was he here right now? This was never how I had imagined it, and I had imagined it often, our reunion, but never under these circumstances.

Sally... He was here because of Sally. I had thought maybe he would be here with his parents and was relieved when he didn't come. The thought of seeing him after all these years made my stomach clench when I thought about it. Seeing him there on the floor, made me want to pass out myself.

I shook my head and rubbed my eyes as if I were seeing a ghost. I wasn't, though, was I? He was here, looking better than he had any right to. Fuck, all of my feeling rushed back into my body, and I could finally breathe. It was as if I hadn't taken a breath in over a decade.

"Hunter! You fucking asshole, help me," Crystal ordered

as she knelt by his side. He was coming to and pulling himself up a little. His eyes found mine and locked onto me. He was as much in shock at seeing me as I was walking in and finding him standing here.

I was by their side in two large strides, and I knelt on the other side of him, my hand reaching carefully down and touching his shoulder. I felt sparks fly from the quick contact and drew my hand away before I set us both on fire.

"Crystal... Hunter? I... Jesus... Fuck... I don't... Sorry. I'm okay... I just," he stuttered, pulling his legs underneath him and sitting up carefully on the floor.

"Are you okay, honey? Jesus Christ, Kris. You sure know how to make an entrance," Crystal's laugh was worried and concerned for him. She always had a soft place in her heart for him. It took her a while to get over what I did to him.

"He always did," I muttered before I could even stop myself.

"It's you..." He glanced at me, casting his eyes downward, and I couldn't tell what I saw in them. Excitement or anger? Maybe regret, for what we had once shared. I wanted to take him in my arms, and I had to put my hands behind my back to stop myself from touching him again. "I... You surprised me," he said breathily.

Crystal gave him her hand, and he gingerly stood back up slowly. He grinned that stupid lopsided grin of his, and I felt the breath leave my body in a spasm as I fought back the urges that rushed through me. Kris was here, in the flesh, and I was at a fucking loss about what to do. All of the things I had imagined if we were to ever meet again rushed through me. I needed to touch him.

Crystal looked from Kris to me and cackled, breaking the reverie that I was lost in. "Holy fucking shit, Kris! I can't believe you are here. I've missed you, you gutter tramp!" He laughed as she took him in her arms and gave him one of her patented bear hugs. She released him and punched him on the arm. "That's for not calling me back."

Kris grimaced. "Yeah, I deserve that. I'm... I missed you, too. I was upset," he said as he darted his eyes over at me quickly, "and I acted like an ass. Eventually, I didn't know how to apologize, I guess." He smiled tightly at her before relaxing into an honest grin. "I missed you too, though. A lot."

"So, you're back in town for how long?" Crystal crossed her arms, studying him seriously as if she was deciding on her next action. With Crystal, it could be anything.

"I'm here until next Sunday. I... Her lawyer called me and told me that I had to come and deal with her estate. She left everything to me, and I have no idea what I'm supposed to do, you know. It's... a little... overwhelming. You look amazing, by the way." Kris walked over and sat down on one of the stools facing us. I could tell that he was trying to not look at me. He must still be pissed. I couldn't blame him, and my face flushed as I stood there stupidly.

"We have to get the gang back together. Danny and Everett are in town, and I think that Wally gets back from his stupid conference today. They'll be so excited to see you. Oh, and I know that Sam will lose his mind! I won't even tell him you're back." She was more excited than I had seen her in a while. Crystal had been devastated when Kris cut everyone out of his life. She knew why he did it, and I was glad that she had apparently let it go. Kris wasn't the problem, I was.

"That... Yeah... That sounds... pretty fucking great actually. I would love it." His smile was so genuine it broke my heart. I wanted him to smile at me like that.

"Where are you staying?" I asked before I could stop myself. I glanced away from him and down at the floor. I could hear Crystal laughed quietly under her breath. She liked seeing me wiggle like a fish on a hook. She knew losing her friend had been my fault, and she had forgiven me long ago, but I think she still enjoyed watching me be utterly uncomfortable. She knew how I still felt. Hell, everyone who knew me did.

"I'm staying at Mrs. Markle's Bed and Breakfast, Hunter," he said in such a succinct tone that the air between us thickened as if it were icy. I shuddered a little as a chill ran up my spine.

"Oh, that's nice," I managed, trying to smile at him and failing miserably. I think I looked constipated.

"That's awesome. She's still as cool as ever. She comes in here quite a bit to catch up and gossip. Oh my God, tonight is going to be fucking epic." Crystal squealed with glee. "You are a sight for these sore eyes, Kris. Seriously, you are exactly what I needed today."

"I have to go in a bit, I have to meet Aunt Sally's caretaker? I'm not sure who the hell that is, though. I guess they're the person who's been taking care of her property or something?" He tilted his head to the side as he looked at Crystal confusedly. "Do you know who that might be. I'm supposed to meet them in front of her house."

"Yeah, I know him. He's standing in front of you right now," Crystal laughed.

"Hunter?" He looked over at me with his mouth agape. "You're the caretaker of Sally's property?"

"Of course, he is. Sally didn't trust anyone more than she did him. He..." Crystal began, but I cut her off.

"I don't have the keys on me, Kris. I'll have to go back home, and there's probably some stuff to show you about the property too. A lot has changed in the last decade," I said colder than I had meant to. He shouldn't have punished his aunt for my mistake. Sally visited him in LA, some, but he never came back here to see her. She didn't even want him to know she was sick. She said she couldn't bear for him to see her this way. I was the only one she let into that part of her life.

"Okay," he answered tentatively. He stuck his bottom lip out a little as he always had when he was in deep contemplation. "I didn't think about it being you. Sorry... Caught me by surprise a little."

"Yeah... I didn't know it was going to be you, either. I saw your parents last weekend, and they didn't say anything. I assumed it was someone from an organization that Sally had donated it to, or that it had sold. She liked her secrets, didn't she?" I shook my head, careful to only look at him from the side of my eye. I couldn't bear to see how he really felt. Damn, I was weak.

"So... I should meet you over at her house in an hour?" he asked timidly as if weren't something he looked forward to.

"Sure. I'll go and get them, and I'll meet you there. It's... It's really good to see you," I managed as I started walking toward the door.

"Well, it's definitely awkward," Crystal laughed.

"It's good to see you too, Hunter," he said quietly as I opened the door and stepped outside.

As I walked, the sidewalk kept threatening to tilt on me. My heart was racing, and I had to sit and put my head between my knees for a bit to try to stop myself from hyperventilating. Kris was here, and it wasn't as I had dreamed about.

I had to tell him before he left. I had to tell him I'd made a mistake.

12

KRIS (PRESENT DAY)

"I can't believe I actually fainted," I groaned as the door shut behind his wide shoulders. He was a hunk when we dated, but he was even hotter now. After all these years, he still made my heart race, even if he once broke it. It was still not complete and probably never would be. That was his fault.

"It was dramatic. I mean, it's something you guys would have expected from me, not you. You were always so steady it was scary, and here you are all these years later, swooning like Scarlett O'Hara. Damn, I have missed you, bitch." She wrapped her arm around me and pulled me to her just like she did all those years ago. We had been there for each other during a difficult time, and a bond like that wasn't easily broken. I had almost lost her, and that memory haunted me as much as it did her.

"It had been a decade, Crystal. He... He has no right to look that damn good," I said stubbornly. "I looked over and saw him, and the room spun right out from underneath me. I've wanted to hate him for so long..."

She chuckled lightly. "After all these years, Kris? After

everything that happened, you still do, don't you?" Her voice held a reverence for what she understood I was feeling, had always felt.

"Does that make me a fool?" I said weakly, my hand reaching up and grasping for hers.

"The worst kind." She laughed sadly.

"You too, Crystal?" I looked over at her and leaned my forehead against her face. "You've never let yourself... Have you?"

"I don't know how..." She kissed my forehead again.

"I really am sorry, Crys... I just didn't know how to deal with everyone after he left me. I was so hurt that I did the only thing I knew to do," I said honestly. I wanted her to know I still cared, that I had never forgotten her and had never stopped loving her. She had been one of my best friends, and I cut her out of my life because I was butt-hurt over Hunter. She had never been the problem. I was the cause of it, and I had forgotten how much I needed her in my life. This trip would hopefully help us heal. It felt as if we were headed down the right path.

"I know. If you remember, I tried to do the same thing. It's easier to withdraw than to deal with what you're feeling. You helped me see that after, well... You know, Kris. You just never gave me the chance to do the same for you." She let me go and walked back behind the counter.

"Sorry, Crys..." I smiled at her.

"I know... You are forgiven. I'm just glad to have you back, even if it is for only a week. You want a coffee?" She asked, leaning onto the counter.

"Yes, please. And for the record, I think you will have me longer than a week. It's good to have you back, too." She grinned back at me. Dammit, I had missed her. I had tried to lock all of the memories of these people I loved away so I wouldn't think about him. It hadn't worked. Every person I had ever dated in LA was compared to them, and they were always found lacking. "Do you own this place now?"

"Yeah. Mom retired, and I bought it from her shortly after I moved back to The Pleasant. It had always been where I wanted to be, so it was an easy choice. Do you like what I've done with the place? I got rid of the breakfast menu and added pastries and baked goods instead. As well as expanded the coffee and tea selections. I make a fucking awesome frappe!" She squealed as she ground the beans for my coffee. "Each cup is now made exclusively by hand. I found my calling even if I'm still a party girl." She stuck her tongue out at me. "Sally told me that you were a hot college professor. I take it you're still single?"

"Yeah," I hid my head in my hands and looked at her through my fingers. "Sadly."

"So's Hunter," she said off-handedly as if it just slipped out accidentally.

"Mmm-hmmm," I smirked. "Let's not do this matchmaker thing, okay. It doesn't matter how I feel, does it? I'm going back to LA soon, and once again, he is staying here. I have to admit, though, I was shocked to learn he was Aunt Sally's caretaker of some kind. Is he a handyman now?"

"Wow... You really have no idea, do you?" she stopped making my coffee and stared at me like I was an alien who had just landed my spaceship in her shop. "Hunter is in charge of The Pleasant's Search and Rescue, now. But as for Sally, well, they never really stopped being friends. She was there for him during all of it. She called him her adopted nephew-in-law. She never really gave up on the idea of you two getting back together."

"Oh, I know that. She used to tell me that she saw Hunter in my future, and I needed to call him. That I was where he was supposed to be, and I had to be the one to make it happen. It got really annoying, eventually, and she finally stopped because she saw how much it upset me." I sighed, leaning onto the cold counter. It felt great against my skin.

She turned back to making my coffee. "So, tell me more about Hunter and Aunt Sally. They were friendly, and he helped her around the house? I still can't believe she kept that a secret from me."

"Honey, she also didn't tell you about her cancer. Sally was a special kind of human and she didn't... Well, Hunter told me she didn't want you to see her that way. She knew if you found out that you would come, and she didn't want that. Not like that anyway. She reserved all that pain and misery for Hunter. He took care of her, doted on her, in the last year. Honestly, Kris, he rarely left her side because she was so sick. He took her to chemo and to all her appointments, sat by her side and held her hand when the pain became to bad. He loved her as much as she loved him." She fiddled around behind the counter and pulled out a cute cup and saucer. "You should forgive him. He's never forgiven himself, and I am tired of watching him carry it around, Kris. He's a very good man, and he deserves some happiness even if it can't be with you. I wish it could be. The torch you carry for him seems to be just as bright, even if it has burned you."

"That ship has sailed, Crystal. I'm not the same man, and apparently, neither is Hunter. I... I didn't know that he had been taking care of Sally. I don't know why I should be surprised, though. They always had adored each other. I know he's a good person, I've always known that, Crystal. I just wish I could understand why he did what he did. Maybe that would stop me from being so mad." I started to stand, but she slid my coffee gently down to me.

"Try it," she rested her chin in her hands as she watched me lift the cup towards my face. It smelled amazing. I sipped and moaned quietly. It tasted even better.

"That, my dear friend, is a fucking fantastic cup of coffee," I grinned.

"You better fucking believe it," Crystal hollered. "Seriously, I cannot wait for all of us to be together tonight. This has made my fucking year!"

I had a sneaking suspicion it was going to be fun too. I also knew it was going to be awkward. Hunter was a temptation, and that scared me. I couldn't let my heart break apart from him again, and I could feel the healed cracks already starting to come apart. Hunter was no longer the boy who hurt me. He was now the man who cared for the person I loved the most in the world.

That changed everything. Maybe Sally was right?

13

HUNTER (THE PAST)

Sally and I talked for days. I had cried on her shoulder so much it was perpetually damp. I had been avoiding Kris' calls as much as I could this week. I had to make this decision myself, and if I talked to him right now, I would jump in my truck and speed towards him. I missed him so bad it hurt my skin. It tingled whenever I thought of him, and my scalp ached. Sally said that was because my nerves were so clenched it was causing me to have shooting pains. I hated it. I hated missing him. I hated that I let my fear stop me from leaving with him two months ago.

I called him last week and told him it was going to be a little longer. The disappointment was heavy over the phone, and it depressed the fuck out of me. Listening to him cry and telling me how much he missed me made me insane. I needed to feel him in my arms and run my fingers through his hair. But I had made my decision, even though now I was making a different one.

I wanted him to have everything he ever wanted without any expectations blocking the large dreams he had for himself. The Pleasant was where I always thought my dreams lived. Now I realized that I was wrong. My dreams were intermingled with Kris' on a molecular level. My dreams, my life was wherever he was, and I could live with that. If we decided to stay in LA after college, I could be happy, as long as I was with him.

Sally insisted on reading my cards before I left. She oohed and aahed over each and every one of them, telling me that she had always been right about us. Our future was to be together, and no matter what Kris and I did, fate would bring us together somehow. I had stopped thinking she made this shit up, by now. I had come to believe in Sally's fortune-telling. In fact, I needed to believe in it.

She walked me to my truck and laughed at the few possessions I had decided to take. I really was leaving my past behind and rushing towards the future that I would have with the man I loved. She kissed me on my cheek and told me to be careful. I watched her wave as I drove away, hoping that the life I chose would be as lucky as the life I was leaving.

Honestly, I didn't know what I was leaving. Sure, I had planned to go to college, but I didn't even know what I wanted to be when I grew up. Kris' ability to make plans and be so sure of himself had always been a block for me about my own. I know I didn't want to be a farmer or work in an office. That wasn't me. Maybe I could be a football coach or someone who was in charge of a construction crew. I craved adventure in the outside world.

Throughout high school, I worked in the summers for The Point Pleasant Chalet as a hiking guide. It was fun, but I knew that couldn't be my career. It was a job for high school students. I also worked as a lifeguard on the beaches whenever the Chalet didn't schedule tours. Once again, I loved it, but that couldn't be my career. That was the problem, I had no direction. My north star had always been Kris. That couldn't remain my constant. I needed something for myself, too.

The drive was beautiful for a while and then boring for a while longer. It felt a lot further than it actually was, which was already long enough. When you leave your home one day and arrive on another, that's a long fucking drive. I thought I would love road trips, I had when I was a kid, but when you're driving alone, it's fucking boring.

I arrived in the late afternoon and found myself sitting in traffic. I couldn't believe it! Who the hell would choose to live in this kind of world? Once I got near Los Angeles, it took me two hours to drive the twenty miles to campus. That sucked.

I had to circle for a while to find parking and eventually found a space on the other side of campus from Kris' dorm. As I walked towards his place on the paper map I had printed off from Sally's computer, I realized that I would probably have to find my own place to live. Kris had a private room, but I wasn't enrolled here this semester. Fuck... Another thing I hadn't thought through, but I would make it work somehow.

The campus was huge but pretty. Lots of green space and old trees lined the spaces between the buildings. Benches sat on the edge of the sidewalk, and squirrels dance up in the trees. It was a small piece of home in some way and made me relax my shoulders a little as I walked.

I found Kris' dorm finally. I was surprised by how easy it was to walk into the small three-story building. I signed my name on the guest sheet and walked up the stairs. What if he wasn't home? I guess I would just sit in front of his door and play a game on my phone. It was towards the end of the day. So maybe I would be lucky.

I opened the door and heard a familiar voice. Kris... So

close. I wanted to jump out and surprise him. But something told me to wait, so I did.

"I can't believe you got the apprenticeship already. That's unheard-of Kris. Seriously, they must really like what they've seen. That award usually goes to a junior or senior. You are going to be so busy we're not going to see much of you." A high pitched nasally voice said excitedly. "I guess that kills our movie nights for the next year. I was... uh... really enjoying them, you know. I like hanging out with you."

Oh, I recognized that tone. That was the whine of someone who was falling in love with my boyfriend. It didn't matter, though. I trusted Kris. He knew who he loved; I had no doubts about that.

"Yeah... I'll miss them too. I guess it's a good thing that my boyfriend decided to wait to come out. It's not like I would really be able to see him, anyway. The professor said this will take up all of my free time that's not spent on class-work. I'm not really sure how I'm going to juggle everything, yet, but I'll figure it out. She said that the person who gets the internship usually keeps it until they graduate. That's four years of being an integral part of the photography studio. I can't let them down, because that's going to look amazing on my resume as well as open doors to most of the major galleries and artists working in Los Angeles. I actually pinched myself when she offered it to me." I heard his keys jingle, and I knew it was now or never. Something stopped me again. It hurt how much I wanted, no needed to run up to him and take him in my arms. I could say I was just here for a quick visit, couldn't I?

Four years? Wouldn't be able to see me? Is that what he said? If I was here, and he couldn't spend time with me, he would start regretting his decision. I knew him. He would choose me, and this sounded like an amazing thing that put him in a place where he was destined to succeed. He was so happy about it. I couldn't let him make the wrong decision. He would choose love, just as I was. I loved him so much, with every fiber of being in my body and soul. I had to let him go so he could soar. I couldn't be the one who stood in his way, even unintentionally. I had to set him free, and if Sally was right and we were meant for each other, life would find a way, wouldn't it?

I couldn't stand to be there any longer. If I didn't turn around and walk back to my car, right now, I would never be able to do what it was I knew I should do.

I ran down the stairs and out of the door. I ran to my car like a demon was at my heels. By the time I turned my car on and backed out of the parking place, I could feel my emotions rushing in. I put the car in park and cried until I couldn't anymore. People looked at me as they walked by, but I ignored them, they meant nothing to me.

My life couldn't be here. Not now. Perhaps, one day, when he had become who was supposed to be, we would find each other again.

I wiped my eyes and drove like a bat of hell out of Los Angeles and back to Point Pleasant, where I belonged. When I knocked on Sally's door, she had pity in her eyes. I fell into her arms and told her everything. All she said was, 'Fate will bring you back together when the time is right.'

14

HUNTER (PRESENT DAY)

Kris was sitting on Sally's porch as I walked up. He wasn't in the porch swing that Sally had loved, knowing him he felt like he didn't deserve to sit there. Sally and I had never spoken about him not coming back to The Pleasant to visit. We both knew the reason, and even though I blamed myself, she never did. She knew he would come back when he was supposed to. That was just her way. Fuck, I missed her terribly.

I waved at him timidly, feeling like a twelve-year-old with a crush. He looked the same but more prepared this time. He smiled that damn lopsided grin, and I could feel my heart race. It was a strained smile, but it was there. I smiled back at him, knowing that it was so big, I must look like a crazy person. He was here, and so was I. Is that what Sally had always envisioned? Would I get a second chance to correct my mistakes? Sally had always said I would, now, finally, this was my chance. I didn't plan on fucking it up.

I dangled the keys to the house in front of me. "Hi Kris," I sighed as I said his name, "I... Have to say that I'm really glad it was you. I guess I should have known it could only be you."

He stood up and leaned against the white pillar that held up the small roof over her porch. "Yeah, I should have known too, I guess. But I never really thought about losing her. I still can't believe she's gone and that she was sick for a year without telling anyone."

"Classic Sally." I shrugged. "She was always thinking of everyone else, instead of herself, always did." I had to fight back the memories from the last year. That wasn't the way I wanted to remember her. Sally was full of life and energy, but the last year watching her become weak and exhausted was a shit-show.

"Thank you, Hunter. I didn't know that you and Sally were... well... You know. I'm glad that she had you here. Crystal told me how much you did for her, and that's... Well, I'm sure that it was hard watching her... go through all of that. I'm not sure I would have been strong enough to handle it. Was that why she didn't tell me?" The smile faded from his face. He had been beating himself up over this. I guess I should have known. It was typical of Kris to take on more than he could handle even when it was too late. I'm sure he regretted not being here for her.

"That wasn't why she didn't tell you, Kris. She knew that you would have rushed here to her side, and I know that you could have done everything that needed to be done. You've always been stronger than you've thought you were. Sally understood that. Remember, she knew you better than you knew yourself." I took a step up towards him and leaned against the other side of the stair's railing. "She didn't want to tell you because- A. She didn't want you to leave the life you built for yourself, and B. I don't think she wanted anyone to see her that way. I was the only one she gave that pleasure to.

I'm glad that I could do that for her. She's been my rock since you left."

"Wait... I didn't leave, Hunter. I mean, sure I left, but I didn't leave everything here behind when I went to LA. I waited for you every day, hoping that today would be the day I would get the call that you were coming. When that... I felt abandoned. Did you know that? Did you know that I spent every night for a year, crying myself to sleep, trying to allow myself to grieve over you so I could move on? You were my rock, and you took that away from me because we were on different paths? I've never understood that." He stared at me and crossed his arms. I opened my mouth to say something, anything to help relieve him of his burden, only to find that I didn't know what to say. I just stared back at him.

"You know what? I'm good... I think I know this place well enough to figure it out. It's fine, Hunter. You can go if you want." He frowned, his brows furrowing as he glared at me.

"I don't want, Kris... There is so much that you don't know." I managed to say even though his hawk stare was making me completely uncomfortable.

"Then tell me! Why did you leave, Hunter?" He took a step towards me.

I wanted to lunge toward him and scoop him up in my arms, smashing my lips into his in the kind of kiss that made words obsolete and only passion important. Instead, I leaned back towards the railing.

"I meant about the house." I looked down at my feet. If I caught his gaze again, I might tell him the truth, and I just wanted to forget about it and start all over. "Kris. What I did... I did, and I can't take it back at this point. I know how much... how much I hurt you... Hurt myself too... But it is in the past. I am not the same man, and neither are you. Can we just start again, please? Is that possible?" I glanced back up at him.

He scoffed and rolled his eyes. "Whatever... It's not like I'm staying here, and we have to figure out how to see each other every day. But this isn't really over, Hunter. I want to have this conversation now that I've seen you. I think you owe me that much." I nodded. My shoulders were up against my ear, and the knots in my neck were spasming. Dammit... Being with him was as stressful as I feared. He wasn't letting me get away with my past. I didn't blame him.

"Before you leave..." I agreed.

"Okay... What do you have to show me that I don't already know?" he uncrossed his arms and gestured towards the door. I walked to the front door and inserted the key and turned. The door creaked open, and I felt him brush by me as he entered. I wanted him to touch me again, craved it even.

"Jesus... It hasn't changed at all," he sighed as he stepped into the foyer and looked around. He slowly walked to the living room. Sally's hospital bed sat in the middle. The couch I had scooted against the wall looked as out of place as the bed. "Okay... Maybe it has changed," he stated sadly, his voice quivering.

"If I had known it was going to be you, I would have taken this out, Kris. Sorry..." I said sincerely enough that he turned around and grasped my arm.

"I know. It was just a shock, that's all. I didn't even think about it before. She couldn't do stairs... Of course." He gripped my arm harder, and I reached out and put my hand on his shoulder.

"Just at the end. She wanted to sleep in her bed as long as she could. I almost brought it down here, but she said it would only be confused. It had been her friend all these years, and there was no reason to make their last days together any worse than they had to be. Classic Sally," I grinned sadly.

"She danced to her own music, that's for sure. Being here... It's... Honestly, it's really messing with me right now. Can you show me what you need to quickly? I'm going to have to come back here tomorrow and try to figure out what it is I'm supposed to do. But I don't think I'm as ready as I thought." He swallowed, and I could see the lump in his throat as he tried to swallow back his emotions. I didn't deserve to see them.

"Yeah. She had the water..." I started, and he grabbed my shoulder and turned me back around.

"Wait! Do you think it's still here, Hunter?" His eyes twinkled with childish wonder. I knew what he meant. I had looked at it often over the years.

I walked over to the large black and white photo that Sally had taken of the Calahumas Mountain Range with her telephoto lens. It was a strikingly large photo with mist hanging on the peaks. She had always said that this photo was a representation of her soul. I reached up and carefully took the framed print off of the wall.

Kris walked over to me, and I could feel his breath against my neck as he crowded in to see the past clearly marked on the wall.

'Kris and Hunter 4ever,' was meticulously scrawled in black marker. Kris' perfect calligraphy shown out at us, even as the sun was slowly setting outside, the room seemed to get brighter. I heard him sigh.

"Crystal said you're single. Has there ever been another, Hunter?" he said lowly, afraid to hear the answer.

"No one has ever gotten a second date... So that would be a no. I tried, but I didn't have my heart to give away any longer." I turned to face him, and he studied me as if I were hung in one of the galleries that he liked to visit. "You?"

"I'm not sure you deserve to know, Hunter. But I am still single, always have been." He snipped but then looked at me soulfully. His large eyes making contact with mine and holding me captive in their gaze. "I still have it?" His breath hit me like a freight train, hot and sweet, and such a heady mixture than I was afraid I might swoon.

"I never got it back," I smiled gently at him. "I didn't want it back."

He turned around and walked back to the door. "Okay. You can tell me about Sally's place later. I don't think I can be in here any longer. The memories are starting to get to me."

I followed him out onto the porch and locked the door back behind me. I offered him the keys, and he held his hand up.

"Maybe you keep them, for now, if you don't mind. Can you meet me back here tomorrow?" he asked, his voice heavy. What had passed between us was getting to him as much as it was to me. At least, that's what I hoped.

"Sure. I'm off, Will I see you tonight? I am positive that Crystal has created a major party for you at the club. It's strange to think you have never been, huh?" I walked off of the porch, and he followed me. We talked about nothing and everything as I walked him back to Mrs. Markle's, and he turned to me and kissed me gently on the cheek.

"For everything you did for Sally." He blushed as he pulled away. I couldn't catch my breath. "Will you come and pick me up tonight? I have no idea where I'm going."

"Of course. Give me your number, and I'll call when I'm coming. Let's say eight?" We exchanged numbers, and as I entered him into my phone, I felt a small sense of hope.

Maybe Sally was right?

Maybe I was just a fool.

15

KRIS (PRESENT DAY)

Why was I trying to look my best? I took a hot shower and stood primping in front of the mirror as if I were going out with Sean Mendes. I kept telling myself that I wanted to look my best because I hadn't seen my friends in almost ten years. But I knew the truth. It was because I would be with Hunter. Damn him.

I could feel the sparks fly between us every time our eyes locked onto each other's, and when he touched me, it was like his fingers were searing into my skin. I probably acted like a fool around him today, but I couldn't help it. It had been him and only him since the first day I met him those many years ago, and no matter how hard I tried, no one I ever met could ever compare to him. He was special, and he was still mine, maybe.

What did that mean? What could it mean? He had a life and a job here in The Pleasant, and I had a career and no life back in LA, didn't I? I mean, I had a house here now, too. Not to mention a gallery that I had to do something with. Could I stay here if Hunter asked me too? I knew the answer, and even after all this time, even with the pain, anger, and regret that he caused me, the answer was a resounding yes. Without an ounce of hesitation, I would.

Okay, so I was putting the cart way before the horse, right now. I needed to slow down and truly think about all of these thoughts and feelings that were flooding into me upon seeing him again. Were they real? Could I trust them or myself right now? More importantly, if I decided to act on them, could I trust him?

Sally thought so. This was her last gift, I know it. She had said that he was my future, and now she was trying to happen it happen. If anyone could do it from the grave, it would be my Aunt Sally. Wise woman...

I walked down the stairs, and Mrs. Markle was curled up in one of the chairs, reading a book and drinking a cup of hot tea. She smiled at me as I descended.

"Can I get you anything, Kris? Would you like some tea, honey?" she asked sweetly. She already had her robe on, and a pair of fluffy slippers sat on the floor beneath the chair.

"No, thank you, Mrs. Markle. I'm just waiting on someone to come and pick me up. Crystal has arranged a get together with everyone tonight to celebrate my return." I sat down on the couch and could feel my face fall. I was edgy, it felt like all of my nerves were standing on end. I hadn't seen them in so many years... Would it still be the same?

"Is it?" she asked simply, cocking one of her eyebrows at me. She put down the Stephen King book she was reading on the little table by the chair.

"Is it what? Sorry, I don't know what you mean," I replied, feeling as if I were being put on the spot.

"A return? Or is it just a visit?" She picked up her teacup and took a quick sip before setting it down again.

I sighed and slumped into the couch. "I don't know."

"Does it matter right now? I know that you had a head full of ambition when you left here, Kris. Honestly, you were one of the most ambitious kids that I ever taught. You knew what it was you wanted, and you went for it with one of the most voracious appetites I ever saw. You always did. I think the question is, are you happy? If so... Or if not... Would you be happier here?" She put her feet down on the floor and leaned towards me. "You know that I knew Sally pretty well. All of us artist types had a weekly get together for years. I know what it was that she had always hoped for, and I think you do too. But that isn't really the question. Sally is gone, and you are still here. So now you have to do what is best for you, Kris. That's what she would really want, you know that. Live in her house, make it your own, or sell it and use the money to improve the life you already have. That choice is yours, and it doesn't matter to anyone but you. Well, maybe Hunter, too." She smiled gently.

"I guess that is another question I have to find the answer to, isn't it? Has Hunter been happy, Mrs. Markle? Part of me hopes that he has, and another part of me, one I don't like very much, hopes that he hasn't been, and I feel guilty about that." I admitted, feeling bad about even voicing these thoughts aloud, and to my old English teacher, at that.

"That's a hard question to answer, Kris. Hunter is content with his job, The Pleasant, and maybe even his life. But happy? No, he has been filled with regret ever since you left. I think it's best if you have this conversation with him, don't you? Perhaps it would clear up everything else running through that artist's mind of yours." She stood up and picked up her teacup.

"Maybe. It could just complicate everything, too." I sank deeper into the couch. My mind was foggy, and now on top of everything else, I had Mrs. Markle's words making me question everything even more.

"Hunter is a very good man. He has had to take over the Search and Rescue ever since his boss retired, and I think he is finding it to be a struggle. Do you remember all of the events that they used to have to raise money for their budget? Hunter hasn't had one, not in the entire time that he's been in charge. He is a great leader for those boys. That I am sure of, but he needs someone by his side to help him navigate those kinds of things. Sally used to shoot a calendar every year and donate the proceeds to them. There used to be a dance and bake sales, but now it looks like it may be too late. I heard that they are in trouble financially. While you're here, maybe you can give him some ideas. Put that artist's mind to use. I think Sally would love that." She walked into the kitchen, and I could hear her set her teacup on the counter. She came back and touched me lightly on the shoulder. "I'm going to turn in, honey. You have your key?"

"Yes, Mrs. Markle. Thank you for talking to me. I will think about it." Damn. I had enough on my plate, didn't I? Now I had to worry about something that had nothing to do with me. But it was for Hunter, and Sally would love me helping them out. Maybe like a last gift from her, in some way.

"Which part, dear?" she laughed as she disappeared down the hallway towards her bedroom. "Tell the kids I said hello."

I sat there, contemplating all of the possibilities as I waited for the one man I had always loved to pick me up. Was he enough to keep me here? Would he even ask me to stay? No... I don't think he would.

16

HUNTER (PRESENT DAY)

I ran home as fast as I could. I put on my tightest t-shirt and threw a sweater over it. I pulled my jeans on and fed Finn. I had decided to drop him off at the station tonight since I had been gone most of the day and was going out tonight too. The boys loved having him, and he preferred to be there than home alone. The guys spoiled him rotten.

We drove over with his tail wagging the whole way. I opened the car door, and he jumped out and ran up to the station door, putting his paws on it, trying to get it to open. He clawed at it, and as I walked up to him, he started running circles around me excitedly. I let him in, and he dashed inside so fast he was a blur.

"Finn, old buddy!" I heard John yell from the kitchen. I walked in to find Finn already getting some pizza crust from John's outstretched hand. Like I said, they spoiled him rotten. "Hey, boss. I thought you weren't in for a few more days. What brings you back here?"

"I'm going out tonight to hang out with some old high school friends that are back in town. I guess you could say we are having a reunion of some kind," I shrugged as I picked a piece of pizza up and took a bite. "You ordered out again?" I said sternly. We couldn't afford this.

"Hey! I bought this pizza with my own money, boss man. So, you owe me a buck for that slice," he teased, but I was glad he wasn't using what little cash we had left for takeout. Maybe I was a shitty boss. Gary would have never let us get in such a dire situation financially. Of course, his wife was the best. She loved to plan a party, so it wasn't like he didn't have someone helping him. Now, it was just me.

"Sorry. I'm a little wound up. My ex showed up in town today, and I am trying to keep my head above water at this point," I said, leaning down and giving Finn a small bite of crust. "You mind watching Finn tonight?"

"I'd love the company, honestly. Finn's my good boy, yes, he is," John said in a baby voice as he rubbed Finn's belly, who had flopped over and demanded as many belly rubs as he could get. My dog was incredulous. "This is Sally's nephew, huh? You okay? I know you're still hung up on the guy. You're not going to like go off the deep end, or anything are you?"

"No. I promise I am cool. I mean, a little fucked up, but I'm keeping it together," I smirked.

"Hey? Did the mayor contact you? He called to chat with you, and I told him you were off. He said he was sending you an email. He didn't sound very happy," John shrugged as he slid another slice of pizza off the box.

"Yeah, I'm sure. He's been at me to do something about bringing money into our budget. I told him that he could help out if he wanted to. Maybe the city could host the fundraiser? I mean, we are the only fire department and rescue department in the city. You would think it would be better funded by the community, right? If they want a fundraiser, then they should throw us one." I sneered. I didn't really mean all of it. I was just annoyed. We did have an operating budget from the city, and that barely covered our pay.

We were only six people, but that added up. When you added in the cost of maintenance, gas, supplies, and everything else, we were about two-hundred-thousand in the negative. I would have to do something about it eventually.

Maybe we could figure out something in May.

How much money could you make from a bake sale?

I could feel my stomach clench as I thought about it. The guys depended on me as much as this town depended on them. I wasn't just one of the guys any longer, I was in charge. If I could keep us afloat this year, I would get promoted to chief, if I wanted it.

It sounded good and made me proud that I was the one chosen, but the responsibility was an oppressing weight that threatened to overwhelm me some days.

Is this really what I wanted?

The only thing I could think about right now was the beautiful man waiting for me to pick him up. I walked into the bathroom and brushed my teeth again, checking myself out in the mirror.

Tonight was the night I made Kris see that I was worth staying here in The Pleasant for. At least that was my hope. I only had a few days to get him to fall back in love with me. He still felt something. He admitted it, kind of.

I high-fived John as I walked back out. "Thanks, buddy," I said as I walked to the door, Finn sat there wagging his tail. I bent down and petted him, letting him lick my face goodbye. "See you tomorrow, buddy."

He ran back into the kitchen. He knew where the pizza was.

He was a smart dog, and I loved him almost more than anything in the world. The man who held the title was waiting for me, and I didn't want to be late.

I texted him and told him I was on my way.

🦋 17 🦋

KRIS (PRESENT DAY)

I got Hunter's text and walked outside and stood on Mrs. Markle's porch. It was a gorgeous night. I had forgotten about The Pleasant's sky. You were lucky to see any stars in Los Angeles because of the light pollution, but here they were out in the multitudes. A plethora of constellations twinkled above me, and I stared at them for so long, I didn't even notice Hunter's arrival until he was just a few feet from me.

"Is it as gorgeous as you remember?" his deep silky voice reverberated through the air and made me shiver. It was much sexier now than it was ten years ago. It was the voice of a man.

I glanced over at him. Fuuuuuck. An incredibly sexy man with the broadest fucking shoulders I had ever seen. He had that perfect V that male models strived for. Hunter had it naturally.

"Actually, I think it's even better. I've spent so many years in the city that I forgot the sky could look like this. It's breathtaking," I said slowly, lost in him.

"So are you." He chuckled. "Are you ready?"

"Yes and no… It's been a long time, and I haven't spoken to them in years. Are they mad at me?" I asked nervously. My stomach was clenched, and I wasn't sure if it was because I was so attracted to Hunter or worried about my friends. Either way, I was a hot mess.

"They were never mad at you, Kris. They knew who to blame," he said sadly. I had never wondered how it had been for him. I was too mad to care about what he might be going through. Part of me was happy that they had given him a hard time. They called… I just never called back. That was on me, not Hunter.

"Come on," I walked down the stairs and looped my hand through his arm. "This should be an interesting night."

We barely spoke on the drive over; I think both of us were still nervous and didn't know exactly what to say to each other. So much time had passed and with it the heartbreak and anger. All that was now left was regret and sadness for what we had once had. Could we find it again?

He pulled up to the gay bar I had never been old enough to go into. Rumors had always been the dream when we were in high school. Hunter and I had tried to get in our senior year and had spectacularly failed as we were turned away at the door. The neon sign blinked, winking at me, welcoming me inside the one place that had always been off-limits to my teenage self.

"Are you ready to have all your childhood fantasies come crashing down?" Hunter laughed at me as I stared at the building. "Don't get your hopes up. When we all finally came here together, we were so excited and then greatly disappointed. It's fun now, though."

"I feel like I am finally being let in on a secret that I have never known. I know it's stupid, but still… Rumors… I always wanted to come here," I smiled stupidly, feeling as if I was way too excited for going to a gay bar. I had been to many, some of the best in the world, actually, but none of them held the wonder and mystery that Rumors had.

"Come on. Trust me, they are all going to lose their minds. Crystal didn't tell Sam, so be prepared for him to flip out on you. Hopefully, he brought his boyfriend, you'll love him." Hunter opened his door and got out of the truck. I followed and stood in front of the door with him. "You ready?" I nodded, and he opened the door. "Ta-da..."

I walked in and showed the guy sitting at the front door my ID. Hunter talked to him for a second while I looked around, marveling at the gaudiness and fabulous tackiness of the place. It was everything and less than I had ever hoped it would be. I loved it.

"BITCH!" Crystal screamed from across the room, and I turned and smiled widely at her, waving back.

"Oh, fucking Christ!" I heard someone say as a blur ran up to me. Sam stood there a few inches from my face, his mouth agape as he stared at me. "Kris? Oh my God... It's really you, Kris?" He reached out and took me in his arms and held me, squeezing me in a hug. "I have missed you so much, my brother."

"I have you too, Sam. I'm sorry... I was an asshole," I whispered into his ear as I wrapped my arms gently around him and held him. It was the best hug. Sam had always been like my little gay brother. He was kind of the mini-me in high school, and even though he was a year behind me, we experienced almost everything together. He had been my best friend, besides Hunter and I had callously cut him out of my life. I was a dick... I didn't like who I had become after Hunter. I just didn't know that until I came back here. These people loved me, and I tried to forget about them because I was angry. Maybe this is what I needed to experience to get back to myself.

I kissed Sam on the cheek. "I...uh... I heard you have a boyfriend I need to meet."

"I am in shock," he pulled away. "And damn, you look amazing. Hi Hunter," Sam winked at him. "So, you two came together?" I could hear the innuendo and tried not to laugh. Same old Sam...

"Holy shit... Danny and Wally, too. Okay, this is getting to be too much." I could feel joy overtake me. These were my people, and seeing them all in one room... Fuck, it made me feel really bad, even though I was excited and full of joy. How could one person have so many fucking emotions running through them at the same time?

Sam led me over to the table. Danny and Wally stood up and walked over to me.

"I wanted to let Sam have his moment," Danny laughed. "Kris, my brother, it has been too long. I've missed you and thought about you so much. I go to LA quite a bit now and wished I knew how to look you up."

"Danny," I pulled him into a hug, and he kissed me on the cheek as he ruffled my hair. "I have missed you too. It's fucking amazing to see you all. And here in Rumors... Jesus."

"Well, I'm glad to see you, but you could have texted a bitch back ten years ago, you know," Wally said, cutting to the chase with that scientific brain of his. I grinned at him.

"Well, I've been a bit of an asshole, everyone. I do owe you all an apology, I do. I just didn't know how to reach out after..." I glanced at Hunter. "Everything happened, and then I waited so long that I felt weird, and... I'm sorry. I've really missed you all. I've never found a better group of friends... I promise that."

"Okay, that'll do," Wally laughed as he grabbed me and almost broke my ribs in a bear hug.

"Drinks, barkeep!" Crystal yelled.

"I'll get them," Hunter said as he ambled up to the bar. I

watched him walk away, and I knew that they were all watching me- watch him. Yeah, it was that kind of friendship that we all had.

"So, you have to meet my boyfriend, Grayson," Sam said excitedly. "Just fuck, I can't believe you walked in that door tonight. Fuck you, Crystal."

"You're welcome," she lifted her glass up in the air.

A large hunky man with silver hair and about twenty years older than us stood up and shook my hand. Damn, he was fine. Sam liked Daddies? I glanced over at him. Yeah, it made sense.

"My boyfriend is in the Bahamas shooting a movie. Have you ever heard of Blake Hudson, the movie star?" Danny said as he sat down.

"Are you fucking kidding me right now?" I gay gasped.

"No, he is not. Blake now lives here at Danny's most of the time. He's just always working these days." Crystal scooted over so I could join her on the bench. I noticed they left a place for Hunter, right beside me. Tricky...

"You and Hunter? How's that going?" Sam said quietly, a hopeful look on his face.

"We haven't killed each other yet." I grinned at them, and they all roared. I glance over at the bar, and Hunter stared at us. I'm sure he knew we were talking about him. "I guess, so far, so good."

"We will talk more about this later," Sam smirked.

"I will say this," Crystal looked over at me and pouted her lips as if she were thinking deeply before delivering the burn.

"Don't you dare..." I grimaced. "I'll never live it down."

"Oh, I dare," she cackled. "Do you know what Kris did when he saw Hunter for the first time?"

"Slapped him?" Danny asked.

"Threw a drink in his face?" Wally said snidely. "I would have."

"What?" Sam asked excitedly.

"Fainted?" Grayson said with a very southern drawl. I could feel the blush rise to my cheeks.

"Ding-ding! Very good Grayson," Crystal winked. She was enjoying this. It was right out of an old movie. I think he even put his hand to his head before he hit the floor."

Everyone laughed, and Danny shook his head happily at me. It was as if we had never been apart. It made me happier than I had been in years.

"Okay... okay... I mean, you can't blame me. Look at him. He's the fucking Hulk. I was scared for my life," I teased as Hunter strutted up with two beers.

"What did I miss?" he said as he slid next to me.

"Kris was telling us stories about Los Angeles," Grayson lied as he smiled at me.

"Damn, you really have become one of us, Grayson," Danny patted him on the back.

"I just don't know how you guys do this on a school night. I have to work tomorrow, and I know you'll shut this place down." Grayson laughed as he took a sip of a drink, I assumed was bourbon.

"I'm under thirty," Crystal laughed as she raised her glass. "Here's to the prodigal son returning home. Even if it is for just a week."

We all clinked our glasses, and we talked throughout the night.

It was nice to be around the people I had always loved. We had been through so much together, and I wanted to catch up with each of them, but we were all laughing and having a great time. We danced a lot. Hunter and I spent the night by each other's side, and it felt so right. I hadn't had this feeling in so long, I had almost forgotten what it could be like.

Before the night was over, Sam cornered me. "What's happening here?" he said concerned.

"I don't know, Sam. It's... been a whirlwind." I answered as honestly as I could. "My brain is in overload, right now."

"Don't break his heart, Kris. Trust me. He won't survive losing you again." Sam leaned in and gave me a quick kiss on the cheek. "If you're not serious about staying here, or having him go to LA with you... Just be careful, okay. He is still so in love with you. It's been like an albatross around his neck."

He got up and left me there alone as the others danced. I caught Hunter's eye, and he wagged his finger at me, beckoning me onto the floor.

My heart leaped, but my mind warned me to be careful.

What did I feel? Fuck. Unless I stayed here, this was going to end badly for everyone, wasn't it?

I had to make a decision, and I couldn't let my heart be the one who decided.

18

HUNTER (PRESENT DAY)

After last night, my mind was in a tail-spin.

It felt like a date even though I know it wasn't.

Sitting beside him, dancing with him and picking him and up and dropping him off... It felt like a date, until the last moment.

He bolted at the end of the evening. I had planned on walking him up to the door and seeing what happened if I tried to kiss him. I thought it was heading in that direction until he quickly said bye and ran from my truck up to the door. I didn't even have a chance to put the car in park before he dashed away like Cinderella at midnight.

When I got home, I poured myself another beer and sat out on my porch, wondering if I did something wrong. I couldn't think of anything that I might have done.

Somehow I slept pretty well, thankfully. I woke up and felt antsy, so I decided to go the station and chop some wood. We have a wood-burning stove there, and the guys never chop enough to stop someone from having to do it fairly often.

It was a beautiful day, warmer than normal, so I took off

my t-shirt and laid it on top of the pile. I loved chopping wood. It was therapeutic for me. Manual labor had always been my go-to whenever I was feeling out of sorts.

I had gotten a good pile going. Every swing of the ax helped to relax the thoughts that kept threatening to overwhelm me. Eventually, I was feeling a lot more at peace.

"Mmm-hmmm," I heard someone clearing their throat, trying to get my attention. John had probably come out to bother me. I rested the ax across my shoulders and turned towards him.

Kris stood there, his eyes wide as he stared at me. His mouth had fallen open a little, and I chuckled at the sight of him. He looked as if he had just... Oh...

I swung the ax and let it sit in the large tree-trunk that we used to store it and walked towards him.

"I didn't realize I was going to find Paul Bunyan behind the firehouse," Kris blushed. I was proud of the way I looked and flexed my chest as I approached him. His face turned a deeper shade. The sweat that I had accumulated from my therapy session glistened in the noon-day sun. "Damn, you are a fucking monster..."

"Good morning, sunshine," I grinned. "I was just taking care of some chores here at the house. Did I miss your call? I left my cell inside."

"No, Crystal said she talked to you this morning and that you would be over here, so I just walked over," he glanced down, letting his eyes slowly graze over my body. Now I could feel myself blushing.

"Uh... Can you? Do you mind putting your shirt on? Those muscles are distracting..." He looked back over his shoulder as if there was something he heard behind him. I made him uncomfortable, and that meant he found me... hot?

I turned around and grabbed my shirt from the pile and slid it over my sweaty body. It clung tight to my torso.

"Better?" I laughed.

"Yeah… It's just I… Well, you know. I don't want this to be harder than it already is," he gestured towards the bench that sat under one of the trees. "Do you mind if we sit?

I walked over to the bench and waited for him. "So, I take it you're leaving?" I tried to sound nonchalant, but it came out sorrowful. I could feel my heart pounding. I couldn't lose him again.

"Eventually. I think so. I stopped by Sally's house today and thought about it. I think it's best if I plan on selling the place eventually. Maybe not right away, but that's where I'm leaning unless I can find a reason not to." He sat down on the bench and stared at the ground, shamefully. He knew that it wasn't the right decision. He had to. What could I do to make him see that?

"What about her studio and gallery space?" I asked, doing my best to keep my voice steady.

"I don't know. I couldn't bear to sell that. Maybe I will donate it to the city so they can start their own small art museum. It would be just as good for tourists, in the end. Honestly, I'm still considering the options on that." He rubbed his hands on his jeans as if he were cold. It was a warm day. Those were nerves I was witnessing.

"So, your life is in LA. I get it. Honestly, I… I guess, I am not surprised," I managed to say without choking on the words.

"Yeah?" he waited, his eyes looking up and catching mine within their brilliant gaze. A moment passed between us. Neither spoke, but the yearning from each of us was palpable. I just wasn't sure what his meant. He decided he couldn't be happy here. His life was somewhere else, and did it matter if I wanted him to stay if we still had all of these feelings between us?

If I took a chance and put my heart out there... I don't think I could stand if he still walked away.

"Okay," I said sadly.

"Okay," he shook his head. His frustration or nerves showing plainly on his face.

"I heard about the station needing a fundraiser, Hunter. I know that Sally used to make a Point Pleasant calendar from her photographs and donated the sales to the station, but I had another idea. I would like to do this for the town and for you guys if you would let me." He stood up and slowly turned around, staring at the mountains in the distance. "It's incredibly beautiful, and I think I might be able to kill two birds with one stone by doing this."

"What does that mean, Kris," I asked, my voice dropping into a barely audible whisper. He turned back towards me and took a step in my direction.

"I need to shoot some photographs for my faculty show-case, and I decided that this beautiful town is exactly what I want to showcase. While I do it, I thought I could take some photos of the search and rescue guys out in the environment that they protect. I already talked to the printer that Sally used, and he said that he would be happy to donate to the cause." He grinned at me. "I really do want to do this, and I know you could use the help. This place is incredibly important to the town, and honestly, I want to do this for you, Hunter."

I ran my fingers through my short hair. The guys would love it. They were all attention whores to begin with. "I don't know, Kris... I mean, when are you leaving? I don't see how you could do all of this in the next few days."

"Trust me, Hunter." He took another step towards me and placed his hand on my forearm. I could feel the electricity spark between us. I wanted to grab him and pull into my sweaty body. He felt it too and quickly let go and took a small step back.

"Fine," I replied. "I've always trusted you, Kris. I always will. Maybe one day, you will trust me too."

"Hunter, I..."

"No, it's okay, Kris. You have to do what you have to do, I get it. Honestly, I do, and I appreciate the help with this. You're right. I really need this, the station and the town need this. Sally would be proud." I said sterner than I meant. My voice had grown cold because my heart was hurting. I was going to lose him again, wasn't I?

"Okay, then. We start tomorrow. Can you meet me tonight? I want to go back and go through some of the things at the house for the rest of the day. I'm using Sally's equipment, and I found everything that I need already. I've been walking around this morning and taking photos, and I have never felt so artistically alive in years." He said excitedly. Yeah, he was on the right path. Listen to him. His art was everything to him, his success...

I nodded. "Sure. Want to grab dinner at The Moosehead?"

"Sounds like a date," he said quickly and blushed. "I mean, sounds great. Text me when you're ready." He turned and walked away.

I picked up the ax and swung it back into the tree trunk.

Happy endings weren't meant for everyone.

19

KRIS (THE PAST)

Between classes, trying to stay in touch with everyone, and this internship, I am burning my eighteen-year-old candle at both ends. It's an amazing experience, but I am so exhausted by the end of the day, I have no social life. My college friends are going to parties and exploring LA, and sometimes I'm a little jealous. Still, the experience I am getting is a once in a lifetime opportunity. Sally is thrilled about it, and a few of the artists I have met know her, of course. Her name does open doors for me. Of course, that doesn't matter much if I can't back it up with my own work. It's better to be your own man than the nephew of someone famous.

I make it home around nine o'clock tonight, and I am beat. One of the campus gallery curators had me in the darkroom developing large prints of some of the featured artists' work for our gift shop. It fulfilled something deep within me being trusted with the artist's work. I made sure that each and every print was perfect before going home. I loved it, and what I was learning and being taught by the darkroom's manager was stuff I wouldn't have learned until my fourth semester.

I ripped my clothes off and pulled on my pajamas. I really should take a bath, but I was exhausted and would do that in the morning.

Before I could crawl under the covers, my phone rang.

I picked it up and smiled before I could stop myself. It was Hunter. I was still a little mad at him for postponing again. I wanted him with me, even if I couldn't see him a lot, just knowing he was here would be comforting.

"Hey, handsome," I said as I put the phone on speaker and laid it down on my nightstand. "What's happening."

"Kris..." His voice sounded strained. I knew that tone. Something was wrong.

"Are you ok?" I asked quickly.

"Not really... How was your day?" he asked. I wished he was here so I could look into his eyes and see what was happening to him. Hunter wasn't very good at hiding his emotions.

"Busy. I just got done with my job. It's amazing, though. I am learning so much that it's going to put me ahead of a lot of the other students. I am still just figuring out how to balance work and school, you know? How's life in The Pleasant?" I asked. I heard his sigh through the phone.

"It's... fine. It would be better if you were here, of course. But I started volunteering a little down at the firehouse. It's... well, I kind of like it." I heard some rustling on his end and rolled over, picking up the phone and laying it on the pillow by my head.

"That's good, I guess. I mean, it gives you something to do while you're waiting to start next semester. Have you seen my parents?" I asked because I hadn't yet told him the news that they had told me.

He breathed heavily into the phone. "No... I haven't seen

THE RITES OF SPRING BREAK

them recently, but Sally told me last time I saw her. I heard that they're moving to Seattle for your dad's job. So that means you won't be coming back here for the holidays, huh?"

"I guess not. I mean, if I don't go wherever they are, they'll never forgive me. But you should come to Seattle for the holidays. Maybe you could come right after Christmas and spend New Year with me," I suggested, glad that we had time to plan this. "It's just this semester, Hunter. You'll be here after that, and we'll figure it out, right?"

"Well..." he said and paused for a bit. I waited. I could feel my heart beating fast. Was he postponing again? "That's what I wanted to talk to you about. It seems that with this new job and everything, you really don't have a lot of time, Kris. Maybe it would be better if I stayed here, so you would be able to focus. I know that's not what you want to hear, but it is how I'm feeling right now."

"No! That's stupid, Hunter. Look, I will quit the job if you come, okay?

"I don't want you to quit... Look, this is your dream, Kris, and it's happening. You are making it happen because that is what you do. I don't want you to stop it or regret it because of me. I couldn't live with myself if you did that. Do you understand?" His voice raised, which was pissing me off.

"You don't get to tell me what it is I choose to do, Hunter. You know that you're the most important thing in my life. If you come here, I will choose you. Look, this is stupid. I just started the job and who knows how it will go. That's not a reason to stay in The Pleasant. Who knows what the future holds?"

"You don't get it. I don't want to be there, Kris. I never did. I was just following you because that's what I've always done. You belong there. I don't," he said passionately. What was he saying? Was this about LA or me?

"Don't say that, Hunter." I could feel the tears building up in my eyes. All of my plans were falling apart for us. "I don't want to be here without you. I don't want to be anywhere without you."

"You don't mean that, Kris," he scoffed. "You were meant for this. You've been planning for it your entire life, and I want you to succeed. I need it as bad as you do. But that's your success, not mine. I still have to find out what it is I want. Who I am. I can't keep being Kris's boyfriend, the football player. I have to do this for me."

"So, what does this mean, Hunter? Are you breaking up with me?" I sobbed, feeling every nerve in my body tighten up as I waited for his answer.

It came with a sob on his end. I heard him crying as he tried to catch his breath, and I let loose with my own tears. It was over. His silence told me everything.

"Yes..." He finally admitted. "I think that we have to, Kris, or we will always wonder if we made the right choice."

I begged. I pleaded. Eventually, I cried myself to sleep, and I tried to never think of him again.

20

KRIS (PRESENT DAY)

Hunter texted me at six and offered to pick me up. I sent him the thumbs up emoji and waited on the front porch. I ran down to the road when I saw him pulling up and jumped in the truck.

"I had totally forgotten about The Moosehead until you mentioned it. I can't wait to finally order the fucking beer burger. Is that completely stupid or what?" I tried to keep it light. If we got onto the subject of the past or us, this evening could go downhill fast, and I wanted us to have a good time. I wanted him to let me help him out of the situation the station found itself in. It was giving me something to focus on, and right now, that was what I needed.

He laughed, and just a few minutes later, we pulled up in front of the restaurant. "It really is right down the street from Mrs. Markle's. A beer burger, huh? I don't think you're big enough to be able to handle one of those." He teased.

"You're so fucking big I bet you eat two," I joked. "Damn... When did you get all those muscles? I mean, you were always and I... but damn... You are a fucking body-builder now. When did that happen?"

"When I started working at the station. They had a gym, and I had quite a bit of anger to work out. I like it, though. I feel like I am in the best condition of my life, and if someone's life is on the line, I am strong enough to be able to handle it, hopefully." He grinned, his bow-shaped, full lips revealing the pristinely white teeth behind. He had always been one of the most gorgeous men I had ever met, now he was in a class all by himself. I wanted to feel what that smooth muscular chest felt like as he lay on top of me. Yeah, this night was going to go downhill quickly.

There was too much sexual tension between us, and it had to break sooner than later. It might as well be tonight. Perhaps that would allow us to move on and see what we might be able to be to each other in the future if we were to have one.

He got out and walked around and opened my door as I struggled with the seatbelt. "Need a hand? Sometimes it sticks."

"No." I tugged on the strap. "Okay... Maybe," I glanced up and grinned at him. His hand moved slowly towards me as he unclicked the lever and released me from the straps stranglehold. "Thanks."

"No problem." He held out his hand, and I took it as I slid down from the truck's seat, feeling my feet hit the hard gravel below. "You look very handsome."

"I noticed you are wearing the tightest sweater you probably own. I think you tried to look your best too." He laughed and shook his head as he held the door for me.

"You wound me. This is just how sweaters fit me now." He put his hand on the small of my back, just like he used to whenever we went anywhere. It always made me feel safe and protected. Of course, it was this kind of protection that broke my heart in the end.

"Whatever, Paul Bunyan." I snipped as I walked up to the

hostess stand. A sign ordered us to choose our own table, so I walked forward and sat down in a booth that looked out onto the tree-lined street and away from the graveled parking lot. I liked a table with a view.

He followed closely behind me. Just being in his presence made me question all of my decisions. I would still give it all up for him, even after all these years. I just knew he would never have the guts to ask me. For all his manliness and show of strength, Hunter had always been weak-willed. He could make his body a virtual temple, but he would never allow his core, his soul, to be strong enough to say what it was he actually wanted.

"So a beer burger, huh?" he asked as the waitress came over with some menus in her hand. "Hey, Sandy. How's Kevin? Is he still taking lessons from Danny?"

She smiled as she laid the menus down in front of us. "Yeah, whenever he has the time. He just made All-state in slalom and downhill, so he's keeping busy. Keeping me busy too. How's the station?"

"Well, we are planning a fundraiser right now, I think. This is my bo... an old friend from high school who's visiting. He's a photographer, and I think he's making us a calendar or something." He grinned at me. "Sandy, this is Kris."

"Hey, hon. Welcome home. I always loved Sally Bolton's yearly calendar she made for the station. It was beautiful. What's your idea?" Sandy smiled broadly at me.

"Hot fireman..." I shrugged.

"Well, holy hell! Sign me up! The Pleasant has a good-looking department, that's' for sure. Hell, every lady in town will be buying one for each of their rooms, and imagine the tourists. They'll love it." She squealed. "What can I get you boys to drink?"

"Oh, we already know what it is we want, Sandy. Two beer burgers with the RedRum Ale, please. It's been a dream of

Kris' ever since he was a kid, so now we are making that come true," Hunter laughed.

Sandy looked at my thin frame and grinned. "Alright, honeys. It's coming up."

"So? Hot firemen? Really? That's your idea?" Hunter crossed his arms.

"Of course, it is. I mean, after seeing you with your shirt off, there really wasn't a question of what we were doing. Are the other guys as fit as you?" I asked, glancing over at Sandy to see how fast that beer was coming.

"No one's as fit as me. But they are all in pretty good shape. We have one who's a little pudgy, but he's handsome. There's only six of us, though, and there are twelve months." He leaned against the table, the veins in his arms popping with his weight. He could crush me with those arms. I really wanted him to... I needed to get my dirty thoughts under control.

"Do you have any reserves that you can call in?" I asked, trying to steer the conversation away from Hunter's body.

"Well, Danny has helped us out before, since he is already on the cities payroll as their head lifeguard and the best skier in town. But he's really the only one. I'm sure he would strip down for you," Hunter laughed huskily, his eyes catching mine and making me catch my breath. I really needed to get over this. He was driving me crazy.

"Oh, I am sure I can get Danny to pose. He's always been willing to rip his shirt off. So that's seven people. The other five months can be group shots. All that matters is we have a hot fireman above every month. Will the other guys have a problem with it?" I asked, hoping the answer was yes. If I were honest, the only one I wanted to train my camera on was Hunter. He could be all twelve months as far as I cared.

"They will be much more excited than me. They are all

exhibitionists. I'm the shy one." His shoulders flexed, and I was mesmerized. "When are we doing this?"

"I think for me to get it done in time, it will have to be tomorrow. Can you get that to happen that quickly?" I asked. He pulled out his phone and sent a text.

"We'll see." His phone beeped. "Well that's quick," A couple more beeps followed. "Danny's in, so is Rhys, and there's two more... Yeah, they will be there. Should I tell them to wear clean underwear?" he teased. "What time?

"Let's say ten." He sent another text.

"That was too easy, wasn't it? I bet that kind of shit doesn't happen in LA. I bet there are lawyers and agents involved, and it takes weeks to get a shoot together." He leaned closer, his kissable face so close yet so far away. I felt brave, and I just let it out. The thoughts that had been in my head all day.

"Hunter? Why can't we get rid of each other?" I asked seriously. "Both of us... We're stuck, and we need to do something about it."

"Okay. Agreed, so what do you propose?" His deep voice made my toes curl.

"I think that I'm not going back to Mrs. Markle's tonight," I said quietly. "Maybe that's what we need? Maybe we never got the chance to work each other out of our systems."

His massive chest rose with his quick breath. "So, you're asking me to take you home and..."

"Fuck me, senseless? Yes." I smiled. "Something has to give Hunter, and I want to, there's no question there, and I know you do too. Why fight it?"

"You really need to eat that fucking burger fast." He growled.

I didn't eat the whole thing, and neither did he. In fact,

we barely touched our food because neither one of us wanted to be there any longer.

He paid, and we scooted out of The Moosehead in a hurry. I don't know how fast he drove back to his place, but it took almost no time at all. He met me and helped me down from the seat and scooped me up.

I felt like a romantic movie star being swept off her feet by the hunky cowboy. He stared me in the eyes as he walked up his pathway and up onto his porch. I felt like a child in his massive arms. He was so strong he didn't even breathe hard as he carried me up the steps.

He managed to get his keys in the lock and threw the door open, carrying me into his house and kicking the door closed with his foot. He was so fucking strong. It turned me the fuck on. He didn't put me down until he got to his bed. He laid me gently down and lay on top of me, his mouth finding mine as his tongue pressed cautiously past my lips.

I ran my hands over his wide shoulders, feeling the muscle that lay beneath. I struggled, trying to pull it off his head. He sat up and ripped it off, throwing it onto the floor. I followed suit. Kicking my pants off as he stood up and did the same.

He was a work of art. Thick muscle covered his torso and his hairless chest made me catch my breath. I looked down and saw the wide appendage that I had remembered hanging down between his legs. The shaft was hardening as he stared at me.

He crawled back onto the bed and his mouth was everywhere. His tongue licked my nipples and my abs as he slowly and sensually made his way down to my cock. He took it in his hand and slowly inserted it in his mouth. He hummed as he swallowed me, his tight lips bobbing up and down as his nose tickled my pubes.

I squirmed. It felt great, but I needed his thick cock in my mouth. I had always thought it was perfect and designed just for me. I crawled on top of him and explored his hard body with my mouth as my hand stroked his hardness.

I enveloped him in my wet mouth and took him all the way down my throat. I relished in his taste, in the musky scent of his pubes and I moaned around his girth. He slowly thrust himself into my mouth and wiggled his hips as I swallowed his length. I could stay here giving him pleasure all night.

But he had other plans.

He pulled me off his cock and rolled me over. His tongue found my hole and he lapped at it before slowly inserting a finger deep inside. He had large hands, larger than the last time we did this. Well, everything about his was bigger. That was not a problem.

After a few minutes of relaxing me, I heard the tear of the condom and felt the cold lube against my hole. I pushed my hips up, giving him the access he wanted as another finger entered me. Fuuuuck...

"Hunter..." I panted. "Please, Hunter... Now." I demanded.

I felt the head of his wide helmet as it pushed against me, slowly finding purchase inside my ass and making my eyes roll back in my head. He was so big...

I put my hands against his chest and after a few minutes of carefully preparing me for his assault, I hung onto him as he had his way with me. He pounded into me with a force that was part angry fuck and another part needful. We had to have this. There was so much unspoken passion and regret that he powered into me. Slamming me over and over, then slow as he pulled all the way out and back in again.

When he came he whimpered into my ear, his hand stroking me to completion as I burst all over my stomach.

We panted, our breath hitching as we slowly came back to

ourselves. He was more than I had ever hoped and all that I had ever needed.

As I lay in his arms, the only thing I could think of, was how could I leave this?

In the end, I knew I would have to.

21

HUNTER (PRESENT DAY)

W as last night a dream? I rolled over and saw him lying next to me. So not a dream?

I think the more realistic question is, was last night a lie? I didn't feel different. Actually, I felt as sure as I had felt since the moment I first saw him. How did he feel? Did he get me out of his system?

I rolled over and touched his cheek. His eyes fluttered open, and I bent down and placed my lips gently against his.

"Morning breath..." He squirmed against me, and I released his lips gently.

"Sorry, is it bad?" I asked, a sad smile spreading across my face.

"Mine. Yours is fine... dammit. Figures..." He sat up and looked sharply at me, his eyes squinting. "Why is everything about you always so perfect. Physically, cause mentally you're still a mess," he laughed huskily, the morning frog still in his voice.

"I think there's a new toothbrush in the bathroom," I offered, sliding to the edge of the bed and standing up. I stretched my arms above my head and groaned.

"Oh, Jesus..." he gasped. "Stop that or we aren't getting anything else done today. Last night was..."

"Magical?" I answered for him. "It was for me."

"It was more than I had ever imagined, Hunter. You are the fucking most beautiful man I have ever seen. You were then, and you still are. We've gotten better at this, though," he laughed. "When we were younger, it was never like that before. I just... Hey! We have to get ready if we're going to do this today. When is everyone supposed to be at the station?"

I felt a chill down my spine. He was getting ready to say something else and thought better of it. I felt as if I had been gut-punched. Was he trying to say goodbye already?

"We have an hour. Overslept a little, maybe. I can go make some coffee real quick if you want." I shrugged, trying to clear my head and focus on the project and not us. I felt as if space had just opened between us, not physically but emotionally. I needed to try to figure out how I could breach it. What did he want?

"Will Crystal deliver? Maybe coffee and some of her baked goods? I need you to get in the shower and shave," he sneered.

"I guess I can't talk you into joining me?" I walked towards the door of the bathroom. "You know to save time."

"That will not save time," he said snidely. "Definitely not. I'm not running away tonight, Hunter. Now go get ready, and I will text Crystal."

I went into the bathroom and turned the water on, letting it get nice and hot before I got in. I was not one of those guys that spent too much time primping. I was a jock at heart, and I let nature be nature most of the time. I did shave, though, like he asked. I knew better than to argue about that.

When I got out, he scooted in. His tight, thin body brushed against mine just enough for me to feel it viscerally.

It made me want to get back in and throw him against the wall as I had my way with him. Last night broke something within me, a dam that I had built up over the years. The walls had collapsed, and the water was rushing in, threatening to flood the deep interiors of my heart.

I left him and walked into the bedroom and got out my typical outfit at the station. I was sure that whatever pictures he would want to take would have some part of our uniform in them, so it didn't really matter, but old habits die hard.

Twenty minutes later, after I sat on the bed and watched him hide his beautiful body away from me in those clothes, we were on our way. I never hated clothes more than I did at that moment. I wished we could have stayed naked together in bed all day. I dropped him off a block away for him to grab his equipment. He said he could get it all himself and would see me in a few.

I pulled into the station and walked inside, Finn greeted me at the door. Danny stood there inside with a shit-eating grin plastered onto his face.

"The boys are getting ready. You know, for a bunch of straight guys, they sure do primp a lot. I think Rhys is plucking his fucking eyebrows," Danny shook his head, his curls bouncing against his head. "So I called Mrs. Markle's this morning to see if Kris needed any help. Apparently, he didn't make it home last night. She said he was probably with you. Did you guys?" He raised his eyebrows. "Are you two... you know?"

"I don't know, Danny," I groaned. "After last night, I'm more confused than before. I have no idea what it is he's thinking. It's maddening. Yesterday morning he told me he was thinking of selling the house and last night he was in my bed. I'm so confused, I can't think straight."

"Sorry, bro. That sounds... fucked. I mean, he seems like

the same old Kris, you know... But it's been ten years, and none of us are really the same, are we? I'm sure he's probably as fucked up as you. Just tell him how you feel. Tell him what happened, Hunter." Danny bent down and scratched Finn's ear who had rolled over so Danny could get his belly. Finn had the life I wished for. Spoiled and loved by everyone.

"Yeah. I should I know... But... Hey, Crystal is supposed to drop by in a few minutes with some coffee and stuff."

"Oh, she's on her way over. She's closing the shop for the day. Said there was no way she was missing this," Danny laughed. "So this should be a riot. Where's Kris?"

"He's getting the stuff from the studio. He should be here in a few," I said before the door flew open.

"Where're all the hot firemen?" Crystal boomed as she carried a large coffee container in her hands. "Danny, can you run out and carry in the trays I brought?"

Crystal brushed past me, and I heard her laughing from the other room as she watched the guys getting ready. Danny and Kris came through the front door shortly after. I had Finn up in my arms and was getting doggy kisses. Kris walked up and rubbed him behind his ear.

"What a cutie! Is he the station dog?" he asked as he made kissy sounds at Finn.

"No, he's mine. He just stays at the station with the guys if I'm gonna be out late," I said in the voice I only reserved for Finn. "Don't you, good boy?"

"You have a dog? Well, that changed everything," he said as he brushed by me. So how do I get to the garage with the trucks? Do you have a helicopter?"

"Through there is the firetruck, and the helicopter is up on the roof. Before you ask, we do not have a pole that we slide down, so don't look for one," I teased. "Do you need any help?"

"Can you get the guys dressed in their fireman's gear? Do you have different outfits for search and rescue?" He was excited. It was great to see him in his creative mindset. It had been a long time since I had seen him in his element.

"T-shirts and shorts in the summer. Parkas and ski suits in the winter." I shrugged. "Not very sexy."

"Oh, you have no idea. Will you send Crystal in to me? I want to see if she wants to be my assistant for the day. And maybe she can bring me in a coffee."

He walked through the door and disappeared into the garage. I sent Crystal with a cup of coffee after him. She was thrilled to be his girl Friday for the day, of course. I knew she was here to laugh at all of us trying to be sexy. I wasn't even sure it would be possible.

The boys and I got dressed in our fireman garb and walked into the garage a few minutes later. Kris had set up a few lights and had his camera on its stand. "Hey, guys. Thanks for doing this."

"Thank you. We really need this. The guys and I would do anything to raise money for the station right now," Rhys said. "This is our home, and we appreciate you doing this for us. Maybe we'll even get some dates this summer," he snorted.

"It's my pleasure," Kris smiled. "So here is what I want. I don't want any of you trying to model, I just want you to be yourselves. Let's start out with a group shot. Hunter, come here."

I walked over, and Kris unbuttoned the buttons on the front of my jacket. I had told the guys to not wear a t-shirt underneath. Kris opened my jacket until he could see my chest. "This is what I want. Unbutton and open the jacket. Crystal will help you if you need it."

"I'm not your goddamned fluffer, boys," she cackled as he walked around helped.

Kris had us climb up on the firetruck. I stood in the door of the cab, my arm thrown over the door, and Danny sat next to me, his jacket pulled off of his shoulders. The others hung onto the side or sat on the top.

Kris worked quickly. He photographed his big shot and finally moved the camera closer, getting us individually and in pairs on the truck. An hour later, he told us we could move on. He took a couple of the guys up onto the roof and shot them on the helicopter. I sat in the kitchen and played with Finn while everyone else got their picture taken.

One by one, the other guys disappeared with Kris and Crystal. They would return back, saying that it was easy, and Kris even showed them the pictures he took. Everyone was really excited by what they had seen. Rhys said we were going to make more money than we ever had before. He way hyped about it.

Eventually, Danny disappeared as Kris took his picture out in front of the beach in his lifeguard gear. That photo would be masturbation material for most of the teens in The Pleasant. He was that popular during the summer.

"Hunter?" Crystal appeared in the doorway. "Kris said it's your turn, and he wants you to bring Finn." I whistled, and Finn jumped off the couch and followed me as I followed Crystal outside and behind the station.

Kris stood there in front of our wood chopping station. "Hey, Hunter. It is your turn. Take your shirt off and chop some wood for me." I did what I was told. I had worked out when the other guys were doing their photos, so my muscles were swollen.

"Damn... That's beautiful," Kris said as he lifted the camera and started taking pictures as I did the same old chore that I did weekly. After a while, I forgot he was even there until I heard him say my name. I had split a chunk of wood and wouldn't have to do it later in the week.

"Hunter? Put the ax on your shoulder and bend it back behind your head," he ordered. It was hot seeing him like this. He was in his element, and watching him work was a pleasure. This was why we weren't together, so he could become this person following his vision.

"Now look at me, Hunter. Right here, in my eyes. That's it," he said as the camera clicked.

Our eyes locked, and he didn't break contact. I felt my mouth part as I drew in a quick breath. The look I gave him was full of longing. I tried to tell him with my eyes how much I loved him and wanted him to stay with me. I wanted him to know that I would leave with him if that's what he wanted. I would do anything to be with him again. To feel his skin every night before I go to bed. To hear his breathing as I slept beside him. To wake up and see that beautiful smile that made me feel complete. His camera captured it all, and finally, he put the camera down. His eyes were still focused on me.

"That... That was perfect... Hunter, you... Thank you. That was perfect." His lips parted, and I thought he was about to say something else. He looked over at Crystal, who nodded at him. "Hunter, can we get one more, please. Can you pick up Finn and cuddle him? If you hold him in front of you, will he kiss your face?"

I picked Finn up and held him under his front legs. He stuck his tongue out and started licking my face. I heard the click of his camera. "Focus on Finn, Hunter." After a few minutes, he asked me to change the pose and cuddle Finn in my arms. The camera kept clicking, and I lost myself in my pup. Finn was easy to love and to be true too. He was loyal, and his unconditional love had made me a better man by being the one who he chose to give it to.

Eventually, Kris put down his camera. It was late in the afternoon, and the sun was already beginning its descent.

"Okay, that's it. I think we have everything that we need." Kris smiled happily. "I'm really proud of this. It's going to look great, and the tourists are going to make you all famous, at least in The Pleasant." Kris laughed.

"Can I see?" I walked over towards him, but he held out his arm to stop me.

"No, sir. Not yet. I know I let the others see, Hunter, because I wanted them to feel comfortable, but I don't want you to see yet, okay? Trust me?"

"Always?"

We all helped him pack up his stuff, and Crystal drove him back to the studio. I stayed there with the guys and had dinner. Finn ran around, getting little bites from their fingers, which he gingerly took from them. All of the boys talked about their shoot and how much fun they had. Danny caught my eye and nodded his head towards the door.

"I think I'm gonna head out. You have plans tonight?" His implication was not missed.

"Don't know... He didn't, uh... say one way or another," I tried to act like it didn't bother me. Danny put his arm around me.

"Trust me, Hunter. The look on his face as he took your picture... It was real. Tell him how you feel. You broke his heart once, remember? Don't make the same stupid mistake again."

"He knows how I feel, Danny. I know he does. I still don't think it's enough, though. I can feel him slipping away through my fingers with every minute we're together." I said sadly. "Honestly, I don't know what to do."

Danny left, and I waited for a while. I didn't hear from him until I went back home. My phone beeped, telling me I had a text.

'I know you expected me to come over tonight. But I'm still developing. C U Tmrw.'

I went straight to bed.

But I didn't have a goods night's sleep. Finn snored beside me as I tossed and turned, thinking about how it would feel when he walked out of my life.

22

HUNTER (THE PAST)

I hung up the phone and ran out of the house. I had to talk to someone, and there was only one person left in town who might understand. Sally and I had gotten close, and she was my lifeboat during this time. It felt selfish for us to not tell Kris about our relationship, but I didn't want him to feel that Sally had deserted him. He was still the most important person in his life. I was just her friend. She had become like my own aunt and not just Kris'.

As I jogged towards her house, the stars looked down on me and judged me harshly. Their glare caught the tears that fell from my cheeks, turning them silver with their silky light. I refused to wipe them, and they fell of their own volition, leaving a trail of grief behind me.

She was waiting on the porch, her arms outstretched, and I flew into them. She made shushing sounds as she held me in her arms, her hands making little circular patterns on my back. She knew. Sally always knew.

Eventually, I pulled myself together. "I... I... I hurt him... I had to tell... tell... him that I was... wasn't coming. That I...

did...didn't want to come. Oh, Sally, it was awful. I had to... Do you... understand? I couldn't be the one... who held him back... He... needs to be free so he can..."

I keened with the built-up anger I had at myself.

"Shhh... honey, it's okay. This too will pass, Hunter. You, who know him better than anyone, even me, you did what you felt was right, honey. He called me and told me. He is heartbroken, and I fear this wound will last for a long time. Only you can heal it, Hunter. I know this. When the time is right, he will come across your path again. I promise." She said calmly. "You poor thing. You would give up your life, and I know he is your life, Hunter, so he can be free to do the great things you've always foreseen for him."

"I had to, Sally. If I would have went there, he would have given it all up to be with me, I know it. He admitted it to me. This is the only way. He has to have the chance to make his dreams come true." I pulled away from her arms and looked into her deep grey eyes. "It's the only thing I've ever wanted was to see him succeed. But for us to be together, when the time is right, I have to know who I am too, don't I?"

"Yes, you, altruistic child..." She reached out and grabbed me by my arm. "You have all this strength and passion inside you, Hunter. You've just let it be dimmed by living in the shadow of everyone else. You deserve the chance to stand on your own the same way you gave Kris his chance. All you have to do is decide to decide, my love. I see walls in you, Hunter. Walls that you have built around yourself to prevent you from ever taking a chance. They have to come down. Your inability to make a decision will one day be your undoing if you can't overcome them. It is the one stumbling block you will have in getting Kris to see the real you when the time is right. Don't let your fear win. Decide."

I spent the night on her couch. Sleep did not come. Her

warning danced throughout my head all night. Decide to decide... decide. I started training at the station the next day and began my online degree in forestry.

But I knew that wasn't what she meant. I just couldn't understand.

🎋 23 🎋

HUNTER (PRESENT DAY)

I woke up the next day with a crick in my neck and my arm asleep from Finn lying in it all night. He rolled over and judged me as I woke him up by moving my arm and shaking it.

"Et Tu, Brute?" I laughed. "You're supposed to be on my side."

I got up and fed him, which made him much happier, and then we went out for a quick walk. I had decided last night that I was going to tell Kris everything. How could we have a future when there was this giant chasm of the past between us. He deserved to know, even if he might not understand.

I texted him. He was at the gallery, but I knew that meant Sally's studio, which was behind it. Kris couldn't walk away from a project and never could. He was probably there all night, finding the right photos for the calendar.

I walked. It was a beautiful day. The sun was shining brightly, and I wondered if we might actually get another cold spell. The flowers were blooming, and so far, they hadn't been wrong this year. Maybe spring had finally sprung after all. Spring break around here was usually chilly. Global warming?

Maybe. Perhaps it was Kris who brought the California sunshine with him?

I found myself in front of Sally's gallery. The walls were bare. That was depressing. She always had some amazing art in there from locals and from her friends who climbed over themselves to showcase here. The tourists that flocked here throughout the year had money, and they liked to spend it in Sally's gallery. The Point Pleasant Art Gallery was a staple. If he left, it would be a generous gift he would give the city.

I walked behind the gallery and saw the little four-room shop that we had helped her create. It was the summer between our sophomore and junior year, and she made us work like dogs through our entire break. We loved it. Sally was easy to be around, and I missed her terribly.

I knocked on the door.

"Come in, Hunter." I heard Kris' muffled voice through the Tibetan door Sally had shipped in from one of her friends who designed it for her. Her house was a hodgepodge of culture too.

I opened the door and found Kris sprawled out on the overly poofy, comfy chair that Sally had bought to sleep in when she was working and didn't feel like going home. I had spent a couple nights in it myself when she had first got sick and refused to stop working. Those were frustrating days.

Kris had a leg thrown over the arm and the under bent underneath him. He had dark circles under his eyes. I was right. He hadn't left here.

"Did you sleep?" I asked as I bent down in front of him.

"Not really," he raised his eyebrows and reached out to stroke my face. "Did you?"

"Not much..." I grimaced.

"I'm sorry. I got caught up in the photos. I don't have much time to make this happen, you know," he shrugged. "I know you were..."

"It's okay, Kris. I would never want to get in the way of your work, you know that. Sally was the same way. She worked in here until I forced her to go home. She kept saying there was so much more to do before she couldn't anymore. It... Well, it was hard to watch. That last day, when she left here... She knew."

"Hunter... I..."

"Don't. It was what I wanted to do for her, Kris. She and I, we shared something special, and it kept us together until the end." I said sadly, my voice heavy with the grief I still felt for her.

"What? Tell me, Hunter," he said sincerely.

I stood up and walked around to the other side of her large table that sat in the middle of her room. It was usually filled with the prints she had taken and marked up with her special pencil for retouches and changes she wanted to make in the development process. I glance down. Kris had done the same thing.

"You," I answered. I could feel the knot in my throat, threatening to choke me. "It was always you, Kris."

"I don't understand..." He put his head in his hands. "I have never... not really. All I know is you chose to leave me, and I wasn't given any real opportunity to change your mind."

"I know."

"So tell me. Now's your chance, Hunter. Help me to know why you made me a miserable wreck, even though you say you never let me go. Tell me, please?" He sat up in the chair and slowly stood up.

"Okay... I... I'll try," I agreed, putting my hands on a photo of Rhys' torso. He did look good. The tourists were going to love him. "Are there any pictures here of me? Can I see them?"

"None of you. Just the group shots and the ones of you and Danny." He slid some photos over to me, and I glanced through them. They were better than I had ever dreamed. He had Sally's eye, maybe even a better one, as she had always said.

"These are... wow. These are really fucking great."

"Yeah... They turned out even better than I had hoped for. I just can't decide which pictures of you. I like the best. My camera loved you. If you wanted to give up being a fireman, I am sure you could get a job as a print model. They all turned out pretty great."

"Nah... That's only because you were the one who took the photos." I gripped the table. "I am so in love with you still, Kris. I've never stopped loving you. When I left... I mean... I never really did."

"That doesn't make much sense to me. I remember you leaving, on a phone call, by the way, and I spent the next year doing nothing but mourning you. I almost dropped out of college. I was this close," he held up his fingers a centimeter apart, "from getting fired from my internship because I couldn't stop crying in the darkroom. You destroyed me, and it took years for me to finally realize you weren't coming back."

"I know... I waited too long like you waited too long to talk to your friends. You didn't know how to begin again."

"Bullshit. That is not the same thing. Why did you break up with me?"

"I was afraid that if I came there, you would choose me over school and work." His jaw dropped, and I could see him swallow back what he wanted to say.

"Really?"

"You... I came to LA, Kris. I was going to surprise you, and before I could jump out from the stairwell at your dorm, I heard you talking to your friend. Some nerdy, thin guy that was totally in love with you, by the way... I heard you tell him that it was good that I wasn't there. You said that you wouldn't have any time for me because the internship and your classes were keeping you so busy."

He stared at me, completely confused. "What? You were there at my dorm?"

"Yeah, I drove all day with my stuff. I couldn't take it any longer, and I had to be with you. Sally read my cards and everything before I left to make sure I would have a safe journey. You know how she was... And when I got there, I heard you say this. What was I supposed to do?"

"Come out of hiding? I don't know, Hunter... You could have given us a chance to work through it. I was eighteen years old... what did I know of time management?"

I chuckled sadly. "Everything... You were the most prepared person I had ever known, Kris. You still are. I heard that, and I decided to go back to The Pleasant, where I knew I belonged and to leave you there where you were meant to be. I was eighteen too, and not as mature as you if you remember. I was kind of a doofus, and somehow you loved me anyway."

"That's true... I can't believe this... I should be really angry at you, you know."

"I do... That's part of the reason I never told you. I... I left you because I was afraid that if I stayed with you, I would hold you back. I was afraid you would choose me over your dream, and I couldn't let that happen, Kris. It was too important. You were too important. I had to give you your chance."

"So what you're saying, Hunter, is we both failed? Your choice of leaving me didn't help me succeed, did it? I am a teacher who hates teaching and an artist who is still struggling to find their voice. How did your choice help either one of us? Are you happy?" He said, his voice rising and his face growing red.

"No... Not really." I admitted.

"So, where does that leave us? Two unhappy people, that

can't get over the past? You took any choice that I had away from me back then. You decided that it was your decision for what was best for me... I... Honestly, Hunter, it just makes me want to hit you." He sat back down in the chair. "I don't know what either of us expected of... all of this. I mean, I have a job in LA, and you are here where you always wanted to be. How did we expect that rekindling our desire would work? It can't... We are both too set in our ways for either one of us to... I mean... What the fuck was Sally thinking?"

"I don't know..." I felt as if all the air had been sucked out of the room. My vision was getting blurry, and the room was starting to spin. I grabbed onto the table and felt the hardwood between my fingertips. My breathing helping me to calm down as I took long slow breaths. Kris stared at me.

"Is that it?" He asked abruptly. "Do you have anything else you want to say to me, Hunter? Because if you do, now is the time. Can you change my mind?"

I looked up at him and saw the fire in his eyes. I was lost. I could feel the nerve pinch in my neck as I tightened. I was stunned. This wasn't how I had wanted it to go.

"I guess I can't," I said. "I know you love me too, Kris."

"And? You know, I do. How is any of this different from ten years ago? Tell me, Hunter?" he said as a tear slid down his cheek. "Tell me now, or it really is too late."

I stood there, unable to speak. MY jaw was so clenched that it hurt.

"That's what I was afraid of...Can you leave? I want to be alone right now."

I turned and walked away.

This time I knew it was over for good.

KRIS (PRESENT DAY)

I was so mad I couldn't stay in the studio any longer. Still, I had to finish this stupid calendar, and sadly the last thing I had to figure out was which picture of Hunter I was going to use. I had planned on making the one of him with the ax, the cover. Honestly, those pictures were so hot, I was surprised they didn't melt the camera. Damn him.

The ones were Finn was a totally different Hunter. That was the boy I had fallen in love with when we were in high school. The way he looks at Finn was just about the most adorable thing I had ever seen.

I scanned through the negatives with my eyepiece and finally marked the one that made shudder when I was taking the pictures. It was the moment he locked eyes with me. He saw me... He always did.

Well, fuck him.

How dare he think that he was my savior. I never needed him to save me from my self. I could have easily figured out how to have a job, classes, and a boyfriend. Christ, we would have lived together. I would have seen him all the time.

Wouldn't I?

It's just like a he-man, like Hunter, to think he gets to decide what's best for me instead of me getting to decide that for myself. He had always been that way. It was one of the reasons I loved him back then. How can I blame him for being exactly who he had always been? Why can he make decisions for me when he was never able to make them for himself?

Why can't he just say it? He won't. And that means I won't either... I can't make a decision if I'm not given the option to decide. Hunter has to give that to me. If he doesn't, he hasn't changed...

Maybe Sally was wrong. I picked up the letters that she had left for me. I pulled them out of my bag last night and laid them on the table, waiting for a sign. I think she would understand why I choose to read both.

I tear open the one the envelope that was blank and pull out the small card from inside and laughed.

'So Hunter is being stubborn. Push him. Do not give up your chance for happiness. He is the one. Choose the other letter, Kris!'

Classic Sally, as Hunter would say. I wiped the tears away with my hand so they wouldn't drop onto the photographs. I picked up the other envelope and went to sit in her chair. I carefully tore it open.

'My dearest nephew,

I know that you opened the other envelope first. Of course, you did. But now you have come to realize that your old aunt might have known what she was talking about. I was very wise in life and now that I have crossed over, even wiser in death.

Listen to your seer, my love. I have never led you astray. You have an old soul, and security has played an important part in your life. Let go and jump off of the cliffs. The wind will catch you, Kris. This, I promise.

If you want to be a teacher, I have no doubt that you can be the best teacher that ever taught a class to see with their inner eye. But I don't believe that path is for you, my love.

You have the heart of a creative and the eye of an artist. Believe it or not, Hunter is very much like you. However, it is his heart that is the artist, and you are his masterpiece. Forgive him his foolish attempt at setting you free. I did, for it was the one decision he made that he felt like he had to. He made it for love. For you.

The heart is a fragile instrument, and I know that you are making the right choice by staying here. My gallery is yours. My home is yours. My heart is forever yours.

Forgive this old woman for not being strong enough to tell you of my illness. I didn't want you to remember me that way. It is a horrible thing to grow ill and frail, and without that man of yours, I would have gone through this alone.

But he would not let me. He has been by my side through the horrors of my demise, and I blessed by the fact that he chose you those many years ago. He still does. He has never let you go, and I know you have never him.

Don't let pride get in the way of your happiness, my child.

Be strong. Be brave. Jump.

Yours Always,

Aunt Sally'

I stared at the letter and let it overwhelm me. Sally was right.

I held the letter against my heart and cried myself to sleep in her comfy chair.

When I awoke, I was groggy and so tired I couldn't stand it. I glanced at my phone. It was only three o'clock. Crystal was still open, and I needed coffee bad. I had been here almost twenty-four hours locked in this room. Perhaps it would be my room one day. But that decision still had to be made.

I got up and stretched my weary body, and walked outside, locking the door behind me.

It was a short walk. Almost everywhere in town was. The birds were chirping, and it was another warm day. My spring break had not been what I was expecting, then again, if it had been my usual, nothing extraordinary would have happened. The pictures I took of the town and the mountains were some of my best work to date. Maybe this is why Sally never left Point Pleasant. She saw what I had failed to realize when I lived here. It was a place of wonder and beauty.

I opened Crystal's door and walked inside. An older lady was reading a newspaper over by the window, an empty coffee cup sat on her table.

"Hey, sunshine! I wondered if I was going to see you today. How did the pictures turn out?" She leaned across the counter and grabbed my hand. "That was a hoot. You want some coffee or tea, honey?"

"Oh god, please..." I sat down on the stool. "I'm just now leaving the studio. Sally really needed to have a coffee maker in there. It was all I could do to walk over. I'm fucking exhausted."

The old lady cackled from behind her newspaper.

I pointed behind me. "What's up with her?" I asked quietly.

"Oh, that's Margaret. You remember the old lady in the big house at the edge of town that never had candy at Halloween?" She pointed to her.

"No way? She's still alive?" I whispered.

"At the end of the world, Margaret will be there ruling the cockroaches, trust me. I kind of love her. She's a total bitch."

She slid a cup of steaming coffee my way, and I picked it up and smelled it, moaning as the aroma hit me.

"Thanks, Crys... I really needed this," I moaned as I brought the steaming liquid to my lips and sipped.

"How did the pictures turn out?" She walked around and sat on the stool beside me. "It was a lot of fun, Kris. Thanks for letting me be a part of it. I'll be your assistant any day, honey."

I chuckled. She had been a lot of help. Crystal was an excellent stylist for an amateur. "You were great, and so are the photos. Hunter and Danny's photos actually sizzle when you look at them."

"I'm sure. How are the rest? I bet Rhys' turned out great too."

"Oh, really. Do you have a little crush? I never took you for a cougar," I laughed, taking another sip of coffee.

"Stop... He can't even go into a bar, yet. But he is pretty." She blushed. "That whole crew is handsome."

"Yeah, all of the pictures turned out great. The calendar is going to be a big hit, I know it. I am sending the files over to the printer in the morning. I need to get this done with, so I can focus on everything else. I'm glad I did it, though. I remember how important they are to the city, and I think it's a great last gift to Sally, you know?" I propped my left arm up on the counter and leaned my head against it. It was heavy, and so were my eyes.

"You've made a decision, haven't you? You're leaving?" She looked at me, crestfallen.

"I don't see how I can stay, but I also don't see how I can go. I'm... it's just fucked up. Hunter came over today and told me the truth, finally about our breakup. Did he ever tell you, why?" I asked, knowing the answer wouldn't really make a difference.

"Yes, eventually. We were all pretty mad at him afterward.

It felt like he deserted you, and he kept his mouth shut for a while. He eventually told Sam, who told everyone. It was stupid, but his heart was in the right place. He loved you so much he let you go," she sighed and reached out and brushed my bangs from my face. "Sometimes people think they are doing the right thing and what they're actually doing... Well, it's not the right thing, and it haunts you for the rest of your life, that knowledge that what you actually did was a stupid mistake."

"You think Hunter knows it was a mistake?" The question hurt. Did I really want to know this answer?

"With every breath. He has punished himself for leaving you ever since your last conversation. Trust me, he has paid his penance time and time again. I think you have too. Did you blame yourself, Kris?" She looked at me sadly.

The old lady cackled behind us.

"Margaret! Keep it down, Jesus!" Crystal screamed and turned back to me. "Sorry..."

I chuckled and glanced behind me. The old lady, Margaret, had lifted her middle finger in the air.

"Of course. I felt like I wasn't enough for him, and I haven't felt like enough for anything ever since. I tried to live my life, but in truth, I was just walking through the motions of it instead of relishing it. We're in our twenties, still. We should be grabbing life by the reins and riding this bitch for as long as we can, right? So why do I feel as if I am using a walker?" I sat up and turned to face her.

"You're still single. Have you never... you know?" I asked, nervous about broaching this conversation. A lot of time had passed between us and the event that threatened to tear us all apart.

"Yeah... It still... I can't get out from under it, Kris. It still suffocates me, sometimes. I don't feel as if I... you know deserve love after that. Wyatt still haunts me. Not literally, of course, but I think about him every day, and I can't seem to move past it." Her eyes started to fill with tears, and I could see her fighting to keep them in check.

"I'm sorry. We don't..."

"No. It's fine. Maybe I need to talk about it. I don't with any of the others because they weren't there. But you were. You know exactly why I did what I did and how that choice led to the disaster that happened." She took her finger and wiped away the tear that fell and ran down her cheek.

"It wasn't your fault, Crys. I was there, I know what happened." I said solemnly, feeling bad that I asked her about him.

"But it feels like it's my fault. It was my choice to not get in that car, Kris." She shook her hair, and her red curls bounced around her face.

"We were drunk, and he was pissed off. Neither one of us really knows why, Crystal. He chose to run to his car and take off. He chose to leave all of us and do what he did. You are not to blame for his death any more than I am, or Danny, or Wally." I said it slowly, hoping my words would help her in some little way. "You aren't the reason he died."

"I know that, Kris. But... I know the reason he was pissed off. I am to blame for that. I'm the reason he got so fucked up and unreasonable. I mean, I didn't know he was going to get that way, but I was still the cause of it." She looked up at me, her eyes full of tears. She was struggling to control the emotions that were threatened to overwhelm her.

"Honey, what?"

"You know how much I loved him, Kris. He was my world and had been since seventh grade. But he asked me... He asked me if I would marry him when we graduated in a year, and I laughed at him. I told him that we were too young, and I wanted to go to college and live my life without being tied down and worried about bills and children. I told him... I said that I wouldn't marry him. I was tipsy, and he surprised me. If he had asked... somewhere else... sometime else... I would have said yes. I know I would have. How can I move on when I know that in the end, his death is firmly placed on me?" She started to cry, her breath hitching with every sob. I placed my hand on her back and pulled her gently into my shoulder.

"That still isn't your fault, Crys. You can't blame yourself for something that happened when we were seventeen years old, honey. You didn't know he would act like that. No one could have. Those were his choices... not yours. We tried to take his keys. We tried so hard. Hell, he almost ran Danny and Hunter over when they tried to get in front of his car to stop him. There was nothing more that we could do."

"Jesus Christ, Crystal. Is that why you keep the poor mailman at a safe distance," an old crackled voice said behind us. "I remember that happening. It's sad when a young person dies that way, but you have to stop blaming yourself for someone else's bad decisions. Of course, you said no. You were a child, and you should have said no, but that doesn't mean you didn't love him. That doesn't mean that you are to blame for his death. I think that blame lies only with one person, and he is no longer here. But you are, and you are in love with someone who is just as mad for you, for some unknown godly reason." She laughed harshly. "Put on your big girl panties, Crystal, and take away the walls that you have put up to protect others from you. You can keep punishing yourself for something that happened all those years ago, or you can learn from it and start allowing yourself to be open to love. You deserve it, girl."

Crystal spun around on her stool and hugged the old lady who wrapped her arms around her and patted her on the back.

"Thanks, Margaret. That means a lot coming from you."

"Yeah... You know I know what I'm talking about, don't

you, girl? We aren't all lucky in love, but we all had our chance. What's interesting is life gives you many more opportunities, if you pay attention. Your chance is somewhere on the street right now, dropping people's mail on the ground or wrinkling your magazines. Don't let him get away."

Margaret let go of her and patted her on the head one more time before she turned and walked out of the café. Crystal wiped her eyes.

"What do you say, Kris? Is she right?" Something about her felt different. Maybe something that one of us said had broken through to her. I know it had me.

Margaret was right.

"I think I have to go find Hunter, don't I?" I said quietly.

"I think I need to close and think about what she said. I do love Larry. He's the mailman... I've been in love with him for a long time now. I have some thinking to do, I guess." She wiped her eyes and smiled sadly at me. "So, are we back? Kris and Crys... the dynamic duo?"

"All he has to do... Yes. I think so. I don't see how I can leave. Fate has pulled me here, and I think for once in my life, I might listen. I really hate teaching..."

"I love you." She threw her arms around me and for the first time in a long time, I knew where home was.

25

HUNTER (PRESENT DAY)

I went home and thought about everything.

Kris was right. I didn't really give us a chance to work it out. I made the decision for both of us and destroyed us in the process. I thought I was doing the right thing, I did. But sometimes what feels right at the time, might still be the wrong decision.

I went back to the studio to find it locked. I peered through the windows to see if he had fallen asleep, but the room was dark.

So was Sally's house. Maybe he had taken off and decided he could finish the project back in Los Angeles? If that's the case, it's already too late, isn't it?

I drove over to Mrs. Markle's and knocked on the door. She opened it with a smile.

"Hunter! It is always a pleasure to see you, honey. I am planning on dropping some cookies off at the station tomorrow. But I don't think I am the person you came to see. Kris isn't here, honey. I figured he was still with you." She leaned against the door gently. Mrs. Markle was getting so old. I needed to remember that I should check on her a little more often.

"No. We, uh... had a little dust-up, and I'm trying to find him before..."

"It's too late? I know, honey. Go get him and don't let him leave. Tell him what he wants to hear." She reached out and patted my arm gently, her old fingers were starting to look a little gnarled with arthritis.

"What's that?" I asked huskily.

She turned and walked back inside. "Search your heart, Hunter. You know." She shut the door gently behind her.

I got back in my car and drove around town. It didn't take long. I saw Crystal cleaning up the coffee shop, but he wasn't there. I scoured the whole town until it finally hit me.

I knew where he was. It was the one place he always went when he was waiting for me.

I drove to the beach and parked my car. I jogged over to where I thought he might be, and saw a pair of legs dangling from the walkway. He was on the bridge. The place where we shared our first kiss. The place we always met at. He was a romantic at heart and always had been. The soul of an artist.

He waved at me as I started my ascent on the small bridge that looked out over The Pleasant's vast lake. Water was all the eye could see except for some mountains in the far distance. It was beautiful. He stood up slowly as I approached him.

"Hi," he said sheepishly. "Sorry, I..."

"No. I'm sorry I... Was an ass," I replied, smiling at him, feeling for the first time that there might be a chance for us.

"Me too. I understand, Hunter. You made the wrong choice, and we've both paid for it long enough, don't you think?" he took a small step towards me.

"I do. I really am sorry that I hurt you. I thought I... I was a fool, Kris. I should have fought harder." I balled my fists up and felt my nails bite into my flesh. I forced my hands to open. The time for guilt had passed.

"So, what are we going to do, Hunter?"

"I will go with you the way I should have a decade ago?" I said seriously. "I never should have stayed here. I should have walked out of that doorway and told you I was there in LA. We would have figured it out. Is it still possible?" I sighed heavily. He grinned at me.

"I don't think so. I think the time for you coming to LA has passed, Hunter." His lips tightened. "Don't you? We're not those people any longer. I'm not anyway."

I leaned back against the railing and felt my face fall. Maybe I had been wrong. Maybe the time really had past for us. I had thought... I was as much as fool as I ever was. I could feel the tears falling down my face. The floodgates had opened.

"Oh no, Hunter... Honey..." He walked towards me quickly and took my face in his hands. The stubble rough against his fingers. "That's not what I meant. What if I'm not in LA?"

I looked at him dumbly, and it hit me. He had made a decision, but it wasn't the one I had expected.

"You mean?" I wiped my eyes with my hand and placed my hands against his as he held my face.

"I am home, Hunter. Now ask me... Please? Ask me what you always wanted to ask me." He smiled at me with that beautiful lopsided grin of his, and my smile replied in kind.

"Will you stay here with me, Kris? I have never wanted anything more than I want this, right now. Then... Forever..." I looked at him longingly and placed my hands against his waist, pulling him into me.

"I thought you would never ask." He said as he leaned in and placed his lips against mine.

Here, in this place where we shared our first kiss. We reignited the flame with the kindling of our past. The fire had never gone out, it had just dimmed with all of the fear and regret that we had placed on top of it. Now it roared to life.

It would never go out again.

MORE FROM SHANE K. MORTON

Pre-order the new series!

BLUEGRASS BOYS
Getting' Lucky In Kentucky
mybook.to/GettinLuckyInKY

A college romance
Enemies to lovers
Anything can happen in a college library

Mason:Being the second-string quarterback for Moray College has its perks. Girls throw themselves at me and I get a free ride to college so I can get my education degree. It pays to be one of the big men on campus. Off-campus is a different story. At a townie party I meet Calvin, who is completely unimpressed by me. I'm not too big a fan of his either at first. But fate forces us to be in each other's life, and with every argument and debate, I can't stop getting this irresistible urge to kiss him. I'm not sure what scares me the most, him or my emotions.

Calvin: Our town lives and dies college sports. These guys get everything they want and barely attend any classes. I work a full-time job at the campus' tutoring facility to put myself through school and I resent those assholes who don't even have to show up. They catch a ball for God's sake! How hard can that be? So, I meet Mason and instantly hate him. But life has a funny way of sticking it to me. I'm assigned to be his English tutor and I have no choice but to be in his space. He isn't quite like all the other himbo football player's on campus, I'll give him that. If he weren't so damn handsome this wouldn't suck so much. But I refuse to fall for another straight boy, no matter how much I want to.

ABOUT SHANE K MORTON

Shane lives in Studio city with his husband and their fur baby, Slayer. His novels include: The Trouble With Off-Campus Housing, Private Waterloos, The Year of the Cock, Fault Lines and The Point Pleasant Holiday Series. His Dark Romance books, written under Sean Azinsalt, include: It's in My Blood as well as Dark Eros. When not writing, Shane can usually be found at a film festival or performing cabaret in a dark dive bar. Join Shane's Facebook Group- Sweet And Salty

UNTITLED

Join- Free Story

Join my Readers Group on Facebook for giveaways and updates! https://www.facebook.com/groups/shanessweetandsalty/

Join the Mailing List and a Point Pleasant Freebie! https://claims.prolificworks.com/free/oXa3gZvB

ALSO BY SHANE K MORTON

THE POINT PLEASANT HOLIDAY SERIES

Something Borrowed Something Boo
A Very Merry Princemas
Cupid, Draw Back Your Beau

Standalones
Adorkable
The Trouble With Off-Campus Housing
Private Waterloos
Fault Lines
The Year of the Cock